Steve Emecz *('Emm-etts')* was born in Lon
the depths of the Australian desert where he spent three months travelling
and returned to his native London where he lives with his wife Sharon.

When he's not writing he likes to travel and work on behalf of his favourite
charity, Leonard Cheshire www.leonard-cheshire.org for whom he ran the New
York Marathon in November 2001. A share of the proceeds of all Steve's
books, in print and e-books go to the charity.

His cult leading character Max Jones crashed onto the scene in 1997 in *'Cut
To The Chase'* and returns in *'Cuban Cut'*.

Steve completed the screenplay for *'Cut To The Chase'* in 2000 for Scottish
Film production company Somerfilm who have taken the option on *'Cuban
Cut'* as well, and are currently seeking approximately $5m in funding for the
first film.

Cut To The Chase

Steve Emecz

First published in 1997 ISBN 190166841X

& 2000 ISBN 190166838X

By Hamilton & Co Publishers, London.

© Copyright 2002 Steve Emecz

3rd Edition - Paperback ISBN 1-904312-01-2

Published in the UK by MX Publishing

1 Clive Close, Potters Bar, Hertfordshire, EN6 2AD

For.............Sharon

Acknowledgements

Without the following people, "Cut To The Chase" would not have given me the joy it has. First on the list is my close friend Bill Butterworth, who experience helped me through the nightmare of editing. The readers, Karen Blanchflower, Debbie Niven , Lisa Ward, Sam Murphy, Andy Holmes, Alex Sanderson among others. Thanks also to Adrian Merrett and Mark Farley.

Press supporters from the start – Syrie Johnson (Evening Standard), Alicia Vella (Barnet Times), Julie Riegal (Watford Observer).

Thanks also to Sarah Cameron and Scott Somerville for making me write the screenplay – one day it will grace the silver screen.......

'..............and that made twenty three. 'Some 'informal'
'nothing-to-do-with-work-or any-form of business whatsoever'
dinner this is. If he mentions the fact that he can do us a nice
deal on our life insurance once more - however subtly,
nonchalantly or unintentionally, I'm going to put that
exquisitely prepared stroganoff over both his inflated head,
and that supposedly quiet, yet overpoweringly loud, Italian suit
- better still I'll just smack him one'.

It had been a tough day. Max had invited this colleague of Jan's
over for dinner simply because it may further the career she
desperately wanted furthered. She is a loving partner, he
granted her that, but what do you do when a bloke like this
comes over and invades the perfectly ordered chaos that their
Thursday evenings are, and have always been. He knew that
this is what marriage is all about. Though he didn't remember

standing at the altar saying 'in sickness and in health and in total and unequivocal boredom while a prat in blue rimmed "designer spectacles" prattles on about the benefits of getting the new BMW 'J' series.'

A pathetic and completely unbelievable excuse later, and Max Jones retired gleefully to his study; spare room upstairs that has a desk in it, to nurse a purely medicinal bottle of scotch. St. Paul's Cathedral. He could see its dome from here. The sun had already disappeared over the jagged London skyline on this evening late in June and Max had had a bad day. It wasn't totally due to the thoroughly unwelcome visitor downstairs. To be completely frank with himself he had messed up. Yes, not for the first time he had pissed off someone that was on the 'Do not, under any circumstances piss anyone on this list off' list. What had begun as a quite ordinary day had turned somewhat sour....

*** *** *** ***

...late as usual, but by a miracle of modern technology (actually less traffic on the north circular road) by a mere twenty minutes. The empty coffee cups piled precariously high in a bin that even the most agreeable of office cleaners refused to venture near to, greeted Max as he stumbled through the door and planted himself behind the large oak desk. Any self-respecting criminal worth his salt would immediately recognise this figure as an undercover policeman. Basically this was because no other vocation allows such an extent of disorganisation from its workforce. Well, they'd be wrong. He was simply one of the most unusual deputy accountants of a hospital this side of the Thames. He had not started out in this line of business, oh no, and it was due to the culmination of events too numerous, onerous and lacking in credibility to mention. If any of them gain relevant status they shall be revealed.

He glared at his 'In' tray. It was full as usual with letters from the 'Compuluv Dating Agency' offering him the perfect partner for the price of a phone call, 'Draino' the miracle all-in-one, house, garden, garage, and cat cleaner, and of course American Express offering a special gift if he introduces a friend to the wonderful world of plastic debt. These he placed carefully (as carefully as you can from nine feet) into the pile in the corner where they nestled quietly on top of an answering machine he had never used, with the rest of the post that had amassed over the last few months.

Around Max the walls were covered with charts, rows of books and the odd picture of the type you find at a car boot sale and find yourself haggling over the price tag of £1.50. Many of them were not Max's but had been left there by the person before, or indeed before that.

A finely tuned mind would have guessed on this evidence that neatness and order didn't play too prominent a part in this burly man's life, and they would be right this time. Having decided that lifting his pen before the morning's fourth cup of coffee was a sin his dishevelled taste buds were in no state to commit, he called to his secretary for his usual brew. It was then that the phone rang. Not an unusual thing for a phone to do, but pretty rare in the case of Max's because he normally left it off the hook to give the impression he was busy. Regretting the first mistake of the day he lifted the receiver.

He could almost smell the caller's aftershave down the line. It was his boss's personal assistant. Despite the fact that the subject in question carried most of the administration of the hospital on his shoulders, Malcolm Pitts was still an A1, numero uno prat. This extensive character assessment Max had put together over the last three years that the 'devils advocate' had been there. Incredibly creeping, energetically irritating, he just wanted to get to the top of the heap. He would get there too, just as soon as the old duffer snuffed it or retired to the seaside with his bucket and spade. All he had to do was keep brown-nosing and succumbing to the boss's every whim.

"Nice to see you in at this early hour Jones" - he never called Max 'Max', it was always 'Jones' - *'egotistical little git'* thought Max, not for the first time.

"You'll actually be doing some work then? I know it's against your religion". (Subtle pause for emphasis) *'..git'* "but we have some extremely important visitors coming into the research lab today. I've sent you a memo with all the details," he added as he put the phone down.

'The NHS has more administrators than patients,' Max thought. He was usually content with the daily task of getting sick people well again. Simple concept, but we are still dealing with one of the largest bureaucratic dinosaurs left in the country. The research centre they had was made up of a few dedicated professors who specialised in rare areas of brain cancer. They were good too. They had found cures and preventative treatment for a number of strains. Still, rather than continue funding this life-saving work, the men behind closed doors at Whitehall were considering turning the place into a research centre for plastic surgery. Not the kind that rebuilt the shattered lives of burns victims but the 'cosmetic' kind. Curiously the transition seemed to have gone on hold the past couple of months. Research that pays for itself they said. Max didn't follow the same train of thought. The only people who would benefit from the new centre would be those with enough

money to pay for treatment themselves. Although not a fervently politically active man, he tended to follow his own personal theory for life - "If you're a little person avoid the foot - if you can make a difference, kick the bureaucratic establishment's ass at every possible opportunity." Not the sort of epitaph you would want on your headstone, but being headstrong and stubborn were among his best qualities.

Sally came in with the coffee. She was OK though. Young, and still harbouring some innocence. No, not in that sense. Naivety takes many forms. Max chuckled to himself as Sally set the coffee neatly on the corner of the desk, smiled and winked at him.

"No messages sweetie," she called as she slipped out of the office. What she was doing here Max couldn't fathom. Her appearance was more akin to the reception of a hairdresser, but she was an excellent secretary and a pretty good sort too.

Max glanced out of his window that overlooked the entrance to the East wing. An extremely important looking car pulled up to the doors. Out of it stepped three men. The first looked up at the grey sky above and shook his head. This and the sunglasses led Max to believe he was an American. The other two dwarfed the first as they formed a miniature 'v' shape and headed toward the large wooden doors. They went straight in as if they owned the place. More evidence that they were from across the water. He notice too that a second car that had been following the first pulled up some way down the street. Its occupants stayed put. Max didn't much like Americans on the whole, especially those in dark suits and sunglasses. Deciding that the day wouldn't be complete until he had executed his personal special blend of red tape, Max got up, carefully retrieving the steaming coffee as he made for the door.

***   ***   ***   ***

Monday. Max awoke displaying an unexpectedly large amount of timidness for a man of his size. The curtain was wide open and rare London sunshine was gushing in. He vaguely remembered the alarm having gone off and hoped that was a nasty dream. Sadly, in a repeat of most Mondays, he had greeted the shrill tones of the alarm with a murmur and a thump of his fist onto the perpetrator of the disturbing noise. Had he been a primed Olympic athlete, getting ready and to work on time from his present state would have been an amicable challenge. As he could not, even in the dimmest of lights, be mistaken for an athletic specimen, he met the prospect of lateness with a shrug and headed to the bathroom. The tiled room that greeted him resembled most of the rest of the house with the predominance of antique objects. Max liked the security that came from familiar things. As he reached for his razor a casual observer may have noticed that it could have graced the parlour of Sweeney Todd it was so well imprinted with the passage of time. Although Max's chin could have been polished off by an electric razor (or even a modern wet blade) in a quarter of the time, the solid brass handle and silver detailing did transform the simple act of shaving into somewhat of a performance. Liberal amounts of balm were required after a quick shower to treat the battle scars inflicted by the monolithic weapon. Within half an hour Max stood at his front door, key in hand with a dreary sky slowly choking what had seemed a buoyant sun. His journey was only really interrupted by a police roadblock conducting random breath testing. *'Good job they don't try mine,* Max thought. The hastily microwaved onion bhaji he'd had for breakfast gave his breath a potency that would make even the least nasally sensitive policeman keel over. To describe the busy London roads to anyone who has sampled them is unnecessary, but for those that haven't the phrase 'Kamikaze pilots in cars' should suffice. Each inch is fought for and Max's car bore many small scars where he and a territorial adversary had pushed stubbornness that little bit too far. Max collected his thoughts and tried to focus on the meeting he was going to be late for. "Oi," he screamed at a bike courier who managed to tweak his mirror with his backside as he careered past.

'No wonder it's the job in London with the worst life expectancy' he thought. He'd been in emergency on a number of occasions when a young lad's mountain bike had been no match for a truck or a bus. The impending meeting didn't ruffle Max as the same rituals seemed to be played out each week. Max would give them the information they'd asked for and by the end of the meeting the various decisions concerning the running of the hospital would have been made and minuted and the tea and biscuits wheeled in. It was uncanny that the decision-makers, stuffy middle managers in the most part, appeared to have their decisions and opinions in the briefcases they brought with them to the meetings. The figures that were displayed by Max did not seem to affect said opinions and thus a heated discussion never ensued. The proceedings went along the lines of 'having one's say in turn' to reassuring choruses of mumbles. He'd often thought how amusing it would be, to him at least, to come to the meeting with two sets of figures. The correct ones would be preceded by laughably false figures which Max would present with solemn sincerity - he could see their faces now. 'A stunned silence befalls the room - the heads turn and looks are thrown at other committee members until, prompted by a tactful elbow, the youngest manager splutters

into voice like an old motorbike on a frosty morning. Two or three of the others try, pathetically, to adapt their rigid ideas to no avail. Then I deliver the second set of figures.

The horn of the car behind him woke Max abruptly from his daydream, the reprimand coming as he hadn't shot off the moment the green light had turned. Although this was one of the things that annoyed Max most - people's inability once behind the wheel of a car to exhibit rational thought and behaviour - his energy was at a low ebb and he put the impatient git out of his mind. Max grabbed another extra strong mint and finding it was the last in the packet, reached for the glove compartment which revealed a dozen or so further packets which constituted about a week's driving supply. He attempted, as ever, to suck the aforementioned mint but soon resigned himself to crunching. By the time he reached the East gates of the hospital, the second packet was almost gone. The sun was peering cautiously through the clouds and the time was twenty past nine. *'Not too bad for a 9am meeting,'* he thought. The porter acknowledged Max's lumbering through the doors with a large grin. The wards looked busy as he walked quickly past the melee of sick, injured and supposedly sick and injured people clogging the corridors. Max's brief journey up to the third floor was marked with many smiles and a few comic taps on watches. Finally reaching the meeting room door he was met by a tea trolley rattling frantically. The trolley was propelled by a small round aged lady whose name was Alice and whose diminutive stature made it look as though the trolley was moving under its own steam.

"Ah gentlemen, it appears that we are blessed with the presence of our learned colleague who we have to thank for a second breakfast while we were waiting". The face behind the voice was small and weasel like. Max grinned an apologetic grin and set his case on the table next to the cold cup of tea that had also awaited his arrival. The room he was in was fairly long and narrow. The centre was occupied by a large sturdy looking table with a dozen chairs seated around it. At the head of the table was the weasel - Alec Farmers - who was tapping his pen impatiently on the table and accompanying himself with intermittent sighs and tuts. His pen was gold, his suit Italian and his ideas somewhere further right than Thatcher. He had been running the hospital a good few years before he was actually given the top job. This was largely due to the influence he exerted through his many business contacts. His P.A. Malcolm sat grinning at his right side. It was Max's privilege to present the costs first as these were then made to seem insignificant in comparison to Farmers' stirring words on profits, expansion and private enterprise. So without much ado

Max got his papers in order and silenced the tapping and rumbling by clearing his throat.

".......and that gentlemen is the future of medicine". Farmers' last words heard so many times before fell largely on deaf ears, though the creepier among those present (led by Malcolm) gave a smattering of applause. The routine over, Max headed for his office.

On opening the door he found the same serenity that greeted him most mornings. In the bustle of the hospital his office remained steadfast in its ability to be quiet and peaceful. Briefcase on desk and mug in hand he re-emerged onto a scene of animated gestures as Sally was in the middle of a telephone conversation. It was quite evident that the person on the other end was taking little or no part in the discussion, as there didn't seem to be any pauses in her speech. She didn't appear to either notice or mind Max's presence until a further minute had seen her voice grow steadily louder, and the phone slammed down rather hard. By then Max was holding two steaming cups of coffee. He handed one of the mugs to the sobbing Sally.

'I bet he's dumped her.'

"Have you finally dumped him?" Max asked

"Yes, he's a complete sod."

'Yep, he's dumped her - here comes the background story.'

"He was just soooo jealous," she sobbed

'In other words, he wasn't liberal minded enough for her to wear less material than a handkerchief to a night-club,' Max thought

"Well a lot of these young men are far too self-conscious," he offered.

"Tell me about it. I don't see a problem with a lycra top and a miniskirt."

'Neither does most of the male population,' Max thought. It seemed amusing to him that while these young guys chased Sally in her various non-imagination provoking outfits, once dating her they decided she needed to cover up. As Saturday night was clubbing night Max had lost count of the weeks that had begun like this.

*** *** *** ***

The young officer moved from the silver lift and passed through a corridor whose bright lights emphasised the dullness of its colour. The sparse design met him at each turn of the winding route until he came to what appeared to be just another panel in the wall. Lifting his foot off the floor he placed the sole against the wall. A small click was followed by the appearance of a small screen. He placed his hand on the screen which lit up. Once it had satisfied itself that the person in front of its wall was appropriate the remainder of the panel disappeared revealing yet another passage. *'Flash bullshit,'* the young man thought. He kept the thought to himself as these walls not only had ears but eyes as well and his lips could always be read. The third door he came to had a simpler opening device - namely a handle, and after a brief series of knocks the young man entered. Although the man on the other side of the room lost twenty years to him it was not difficult to see that his physique and frame matched his. He had his back to the door and was looking at a map screen of some sort located on the back wall.

"Sit down Easton," he said without turning around. His voice was deep and a little melancholy. The younger man sat with his arms crossed and the folder he had brought with him on his lap. His cap hid most of his dark hair which was cropped very short. Still without turning around, as if to add emphasis, his superior continued.

"As you have no doubt digested everything in that file, I'll cut to the chase. Although this may seem a cushy assignment on the surface - baby-sitting a few scientists and surgeons - you will have noted it is marked with a code 3. Why this is the case, is of little concern to me and will be of none to you. But it is there for a reason. You should feel honoured to get something like this after only a few years with us."

'Oh great, a month in dreary London watching over a bunch of eggheads,' thought the young man as he let his eyes drift to the map on the screen.

"If this goes without a hitch I'll recommend they push you up a couple of levels," the older man said as he turned around. His face was suitably worn and hardened with a few noticeable scars. Easton could almost imagine the man in front of him with M16 in hand, tramping though the jungles of North Korea or Vietnam. Although he never mentioned the above conflicts it was widely known that he had been decorated for his conduct in both.

"Your name is now Sherman Jeffries and you are with the Institute of Medicine of New England. Considering you studied medicine next to law you should be able to carry that one off. You have a wife and a two-year-old son called James. All your papers and personal effects are in the package on the desk. As your file states you will be in London for a month, though this could be extended."

"Extended?" asked Easton surprised.

"Yes, extended. Due to the medical nature of the operation, no pun intended, it could take longer."

"May I ask how much longer?"

"You may, but as my medical expertise doesn't stretch past basic first aid you are unlikely to get a straight answer."

'Great, so I could be stuck there for months,' he mused.

"I know what you're thinking, that this is a real piece of crap to be thrown, but our work isn't restricted to terrorists and revolutionaries. At least you'll not be dodging bullets and sleeping in ditches," he grinned.

"One question Sir. The file mentions a partner. Am I at liberty to know who I will be going with?"

"Oh you'll find out on the plane - its in the package. Don't panic, you know him quite well."

At this, he handed the package to the young officer, who took this as the sign that the brief meeting was over. He saluted his superior and with the file and package lodged under his arm he ventured into the corridor once more.

***   ***   ***   ***

The kickback from the Baretta pistol felt good in his right hand as he pummelled half a dozen bullets into the approaching soldier before ducking behind the low stone wall off to his left. The cold air drifted over his face as he paused, making him aware of the beads of sweat slipping down his brow. Counting to three he threw himself to the ground six feet away and released the remaining bullets into the second figure. A mortar exploded somewhere behind him and showered him in earth. It took a split second for his eyes to adjust in the smoke. Scanning the horizon for a moment he located the awaiting transport and broke into a sprint. He discovered another enemy in the boggy earth but somehow he managed to vault the ramshackle fence in his way. Only a few yards to go and suddenly he felt a thud in his right shoulder. Looking down he saw the yellow patch and swore out loud. The run slowed to a walk and he approached Major Hava with a stern expression.

"Sniper you fool!" screamed the major as he got within six feet. "Apart from missing him in sector two the rest was pretty good….for a lard-ass agency nancy-boy," he sneered as his old friend saluted and handed over the weapon for inspection. Anders smiled and climbed into the jeep. It felt damn good to keep his skills up. Although the training facility was mandatory for all operatives once a year, he found himself back in Hawksville every few months. He was annoyed at having missed the presence of the sniper cut-out, but had hit every other target on the range. The adrenaline rush had been severely lacking in the last few assignments and he wondered if the next one would contain any excitement.

*** *** *** ***

Tuesday. Max took a long gulp of his steaming coffee. Between his mint addiction and preference for boiling drinks he had assumed his taste buds would disappear completely before he reached thirty. That hadn't happened and Max often pictured them as armour-plated. Sally had not touched her coffee yet and was at the kettle making him a second cup. As he stepped into the main office he exchanged a pile of typing for the aforementioned coffee and returned to his desk. Any visitor to his office would find Max's door open at all times. If the door was shut it meant he was out. From the doorway you could see a huge desk dominating the centre of the room and around the edges various office machinery, each with a pile of paper covering it. Max's theory here was that no dust could collect on said equipment if they were shrouded with paper. He of course knew exactly where everything was, but to the casual observer the scene was one of cosy disorder. On his desk was a PC which hid within its dull grey casing how organised this man really was. Despite being apathetic toward the dreaded machines for many years Max became computer literate with a vengeance with the advent of the 'stand-alone' PC. Although it was linked, for certain applications, with the hospital's mainframe and a local network inside his department, what lived on his PC was largely his business and that's the way Max liked it. Rumours abounded within the hospital of his computer skills but one visit to his messy office was usually enough to dispel these. In case of further prying eyes Max had installed an intricate protection system that in an establishment like St. Mary's was vastly over the top. It was more for his peace of mind than serving any functional value. However, hidden behind the mass of codes and passwords were files containing Max's figurework on the running costs of the place since he had been there. They showed the current boss in a very unfavourable light. Farmers had massaged the figures for a number of years. Max kept these as security for the time when he might need them. Farmers didn't like Max and on the occasions Max had stood against his wayward ideas on the grounds of common sense he had warned him that his days were numbered. Max knew, for instance, that the investment from the Italians three years before had been an unmitigated disaster. The true costs had been hidden and Farmers had come out of the fiasco without a mark. Max had been the first to push for, and get CD Roms in to the department. His PC also had a removable hard-drive of which he had two backups. On the hospital records only one of those was shown. The other lived in a post office box in his uncle's hometown of Melksham. Now this may seem a little paranoid, or at the very least over cautious, but Max was familiar with Farmers' methods. Many a member of staff in his way had been given the bullet prematurely. Max liked this job and no little jumped up git in an Italian suit was going to take it away from him. In true tradition though, Max left the PC undusted and the desk uncleared. This further fuelled the impression that the machine was there for occasional use and nothing else. He was sitting beside the PC working on his notes from yesterday's meeting. Though the sun was still fighting a losing battle with the clouds the office was fairly bright.

*** *** *** ***

Matheson air force base....10:30pm. Two figures are walking across the tarmac towards a transport plane. Their silhouettes against the myriad of lights inside the control tower reveal one is slightly shorter than the other and they are both carrying large bags. The back of the plane is open and the two figures, both silent, disappear into the belly of the plane. The plane makes one stop-off at JFK to pick up fuel and it is there that the two figures re-emerge, minus the caps and bags. The younger man has short dark hair, deep blue eyes and is wearing a very plain grey suit which looks out of place on his shoulders. The taller man is perhaps fifteen years older with a face that nature had not been altogether generous to. The passage of the last twenty years is imbedded in the stern wrinkles and furrowed brow. He doesn't smile and his eyes are hidden by mirrored sunglasses despite the fact that it is the middle of the night. He, too, is wearing a conservative suit and they look like two businessmen about to board a commuter train into the city.

'I'm determined not to mention the sunglasses,' Easton thought. *'He's bound to give me a lecture, but he couldn't be less conspicuous if his hair was green.'*

"The sunglasses are fine - it means that people think my eyesight is impaired and that gives me another edge."

'Gees was this guy telepathic or what. Nope, it was me looking over out of the corner of my eye.' He tried to change the subject.

"You looking forward to London?" he asked as enthusiastically as he could muster.

"Oh sure, I get two lots of baby-sitting this time," came the terse reply.

'I ought to know better. If he's quite happy to act like a monk I guess I shouldn't bother to try and make conversation,' Easton thought and turned his thoughts toward breakfast. This was the fourth time he'd been paired with Anders and he had yet to shake off the 'rookie' tag. You had to respect the man. More senior, more skilled, and still alive at the age of forty-five in a profession where the odds were heavily stacked against growing to a ripe old age. Nevertheless, Easton was frustrated

at being treated like a kid. He was damn good. Why else was he where he was by the age of thirty. But that didn't count for anything with Anders, oh no. You had to have survived at the hands of the PLO, had a number of near fatal wounds and lost a finger, toe, testicle or earlobe during either warfare or torture of some description. He had to admit that the previous three missions they had been paired together had been fairly routine and had gone almost to plan. The exception had been the last one, where Easton had almost been caught. A fact Anders would never let him forget. He had been standing by the swimming pool and had watched Easton's premature exit from the hotel room's second floor window. The hotel had been in Jakarta, and the impromptu exit due to a double-cross by their contact there. They entered the domestic terminal via an inconspicuous door near to baggage claim and went to the bar. Four hours later a bus took them to the international terminal and flight BA127 to London Heathrow.

***   ***   ***   ***

Thursday. It had been an uneventful afternoon and the sun had almost decided to call it a day. Max stared at the computer sheet on his desk. The yellow highlighted figures stared back at him. Part of him wanted to just add a few notes and slip it into

Dr Reimer's tray. He would get it back in a couple of days later with a plausible reason the cost committee would be happy with. Another part, the stronger part, was angered by the channelling of funds into the research centre. Decision made, Max got up and walked to the photocopier by the window. All cost rises of 40% or more were highlighted and this week's list had twenty of them. As the copier kicked into life he glanced out over the car park. How the face of the hospital had changed over the last twelve months. The plush new wing with its fancy security system, wards that look more like hotel rooms. "…This is the future of British medicine - private research will fund an increased level of patient care." Farmers' words as he had cut the tape at its opening still clear in Max's memory. The lights were all out but the dim glow of all manner of computer wizardry at rest lit the parking places outside. There always seemed to be plenty of cars at night too. Probably all the commissioned professors working through the night researching the next breakthrough in plastic surgery. Max chuckled to himself as he pictured a life-size Barbie doll sitting behind the reception. He slipped the copy back into the folder and the original into the bottom drawer.

There is an uneasy quiet that people associate with hospitals after dark. As Max walked the stairs and corridors toward the new wing, the small hives of activity that surrounded the sisters going about their duties were like oases in a dreary desert. Peaceful though. Max liked this time of the day. There wasn't that same air of illness or presence of suffering. The bleachy smell was the same but Max was almost immune to that by now. He reached the security doors and was greeted by a pleasant grin.

"Hiya Max. They sure got you tied to you're desk these days."

"Merv. When's the next shipment of rum coming from your brother?" Merv had the best Jamaican connections in North London and could get the best rum this side of Kingston Town.

"Next week man. Don't tell me you drunk those two bottles already," he chuckled.

"Almost," said Max as he ran his pass through the decoder.

"I need to do a bunch of sections this week. We're really up against it with the end of the budget this month." Although he knew exactly where he wanted to go, Max went through the motions of pulling the sheet from the folder. Merv was a long-standing part of St. Mary's and he and Max had always got on well. They shared the same taste in rum. Max shuffled the sheets and read out as he came to each new section.

"Hey, you know I can't get you into G section - you can leave that one with me and I'll get Dr.Reimer to sort it out for you tomorrow," Merv said.

"Oh OK," Max replied shutting the folder and walking towards the inner door.

"Shit, I almost forgot. Dr Reimer wants these figures typed by Monday. Any chance you can swing the section for me. It'll only take a minute," Max pleaded.

"Well I'm not sure…" Merv said contemplating the idea.

"You can come with me if you like?" Max offered.

"OK, I'll get Barry to take over here," Merv smiled.

Merv was small for what Max assumed, judging by other acquaintances, the average size of Jamaicans is. His beard was short and liberally specked with grey. The grey had yet to reach his hair, which was still as dark as coal. Max suspected that this wasn't entirely due to strong follicles. He looked fairly distinguished in his 'mock policeman's' uniform that all security staff had to wear. *'Under duress,'* Max thought. Merv was quickly relieved by Barry who in contrast was a plain, expressionless, thin, tall man with whom a long discussion was limited to a couple of sentences. An avid collector of dead insects apparently. *'Wouldn't surprise me,'* Max thought as his smile was returned by a forced blank grin that seemed to defy all the other muscles in the young man's face. Max followed Merv through the buzz of the security door and down a long brightly lit corridor.

"I remember when this was a children's ward," mumbled Max.

"Yep, sure is quieter," laughed Merv, "but it hasn't got no life any more - unless you call them machines a'clickin and a whirrin all night lively," he frowned.

"I bet even Barry gets bored with this," said Max.

"Hmm, difficult to tell, man," replied Merv as he slid his security card through another door lock. The card was met with a small beep and a green light. *'Star bloody Trek,'* Max thought as the door panned slowly back to reveal a smaller corridor with three doors either side in perfect symmetry. The floors and walls were a dark grey and the door frames only a marginally lighter shade. A far cry from the plush, plant-dominated reception area and the private rooms that the punters actually got to see. Max remembered back to his visits to RAF Morton and expected his friend Carl to greet them as Merv threw the latch on one of the doors. The innards of this fortress were little different to other labs Max had seen on his travels. More attention to detail perhaps. The main lights were on, possibly triggered by the lock. Everything was bathed in a sharp white light. *'It probably looks the same in the daytime,'* Max thought as he walked to the first storage unit and checked its contents. There was something macabre in the organs encased in their various containers. Of course they weren't visible but Max could see their images in the wording on the labels. He supposed that once you've seen more livers than a Pavarotti fry up of a morning, then it was natural for the mind to override the weaker sense and allow such a deeper sight. In much the same way his neighbour Daniel was able to evoke Max's taste buds with the most graphic descriptions of a gourmet meal he had recently prepared. Max slowly redressed the whiteness of the page with strokes from his red highlighter as the resting places and uses of the various stocks revealed themselves in the cabinets. With all but one of the items on the list checked Max motioned that yet another door needed opening. Merv handed him the pass without moving from the stool he had found. His distant gaze didn't alter as Max opened the thick metal door that was marked only with the letters B.R.I. The door opened not onto another room but a small storage area. Its walls were sliding doors of glass. Max quickly identified where the substance had been employed and noted the relevant details against the text on the sheet.

'I expect they'll put bar codes on these one day,' Max thought as he compared the shelves to those in his local supermarket. The inner door clicked shut and Max made a low rumble in his throat which stirred Merv from his gazing into space.

"On the beach again?" Max whispered as Merv clicked open the door.

"Yep, with me rum bottle sittin in the ice bucket and the young ladies playing volleyball in the sun," he grinned revealing a row of white teeth a man half his age would be proud of.

"Just another three years," he added.

"As few as that. You make me feel old," Max laughed.

"Not so much of the old you young puppy. 'Experienced' is a far better word," Merv laughed.

"Well, save me a deck-chair," Max shouted over his shoulder as he passed through the final door manned by the ever alert Barry.

As Max turned the key in his office door he thought of his impending drive home, no traffic but plenty of roadworks. It was a matter of minutes before he'd keyed in the necessary details. It would be flattery to describe him as a touch typist but a number of years in front of the 'infernal machines' had quickened his pace. As he went through Max corrected any obvious mistakes in spelling etc. *'Sally's had a bad week,'* he said to himself. The young lady in question, he remembered, was having another man crisis and her attention was wavering. Three d's in acidic did seem a touch excessive. She had even left out the date when Mr. Verdkyll had passed away, but seeing as the tissue that occupied his jar in the lab was less than 24 hrs old Max keyed in "Thursday 10pm" as a rough guess. *'That way she won't get dragged over the coals on Monday,'* mumbled Max to himself as he put the papers in his top drawer and silenced the computer with the flick of a switch. *'Maybe then I'll have a quiet start to the week instead of tears and woe with my first cup of coffee,'* he thought.

*** *** *** ***

"Get that bloody smile off your face missy...!"

The large woman behind the voice was Sister Mary, and everyone knew it. Her request, or rather order, was directed at a young nurse on the opposite side of the bed. The nurse's red hair was straight, long and cascaded over her shoulders when it was loose but on duty was tied into a neat bun. She had a natural gleam in her green eyes, which incidentally went with her hair to a tee.

"You know Mr.Mortimer needs stern treatment," the sister continued.

'Or neutering,' thought Kathy.

"Yes Sister," she said as if the last comment had been an order too. To this the sister gave an indignant 'humph', spun on her heels and headed down the ward looking for the next victim of her sharp tongue. Mr Mortimer was almost a regular. He had a tiny feeble five foot four frame but caused most of the commotion on the ward. He suffered from an endless stream of minor strokes, and while in the hospital dealt out his fair share of strokes too. Student nurses screamed, doctors tutted and the rest of the onlookers were usually quite amused. Kathy could handle him though. She referred to him as being in his 'second adolescence'. His frown was still there as she looked at him.

"My arms are too short and your bum's too small," he complained

"Thank you for the compliment, I think," she smiled. She gave him his pills, he refused. She finally got him to take them by telling him they were hallucinogenic drugs. Had his memory been better he would have remembered her using the same trick a few days earlier. She'd had a ticking off from the sister to whom Mr.Mortimer had complained that his LSD fixes hadn't worked properly. Kathy looked to her left and saw the 'old battle-axe' taking a piece out of Max. She liked Max. He was down to earth and funny. Now if he were ten years younger, half the size and looked different then there'd be no stopping her. It was rumoured that Sister Mary had a soft spot for him. *'That narrows it down to almost any part of her anatomy'* Kathy thought. She saw his eyes dart in her direction, as if a cry for help. She smiled and walked over to the animated sister and interrupted.

"Oh Max, I've got some urgent paperwork from Dr. Coulemans for you."

"Ah yes," Max said feigning urgency.

"I've been waiting for that, can I come and get it now?" he said.

'Sharp as ever,' thought Kathy.

'Wonderful,' thought Max.

"Of course, I'll take you through," Kathy said grabbing his arm quickly before Sister Mary could open her mouth again.

They scuttled off down the ward and into a quiet corridor and slowed to a walking pace.

"Thanks," said Max

"Oh, just my good deed for the day," she replied in the soft Welsh accent he liked so much.

"You know she fancies you...?" she continued with a grin.

"Hmm," he frowned "I had hoped that was a vicious rumour spread by an enemy bent on revenge," he said breaking into a smile.

" 'Fraid not. Anyway, how are things, I haven't seen you down here for a few days."

"I'm sorry, I've had so much extra figurework. That new research centre generates more hassle than the rest of the place put together."

"I guess it does," she said. There was that smile again.

'*I must change the subject*' Max thought as he felt himself staring at her eyes.

"Anything much happen this week?"

"Not much. Mr Mortimer is back again so Sister Mary is being a pain. There's a new young doctor, no he's not my type, and we lost Mr.Verdkyll."

" Ah yes, rather sad that," Max said trying to sound sincere even though he hadn't known the man personally.

"Yes, he had been battling cancer for two years, always bubbly and friendly."

"Cancer?" Max stopped in his tracks.

"Yes, lung cancer," Kathy repeated looking puzzled.

"Why do you ask?"

"Oh nothing, just that one of the patients in the neural section had a similar name and also died on Thursday."

"Can't be the same one then, Mr.Verdkyll didn't die until Saturday. Well, they turned his machine off with his wife's permission. The son was there too, very sad."

"Must be a different chap," said Max dismissing the point.

"So, you free for lunch?" he asked hopefully

"My my, you don't come and visit me for a week and then expect lunch. Well I might be in the canteen at one, and if there aren't any other free tables I might just sit next to you," she smiled.

"Why thank you," Max grinned and pushed through the doors into X-Ray.

*** *** *** ***

The doors on the conference room clicked to a close and the short man reached for the phone and dialled the number. After a series of clicks a voice came on the other end.

"Yes. I told you never to call me at this number unless it was serious," the voice snapped.

The short man glanced at the closed door.

"Yes well, I think it is. One of the staff has been nosing around our research area," he said quietly.

"What, a doctor you mean?" the voice answered concerned.

"No, an accountant. Jones" replied the short man.

"And that worries you? Very well, I'll deal with it. We can't take any chances with what is at stake. Not a word to our two boys. We don't want them knowing any more than absolutely necessary. Right?"

"Yessir," the short man replied and slowly replaced the handset. He looked out of the window across to Jones' office and felt a pang of guilt. Was he being too cautious or was there really a danger that he would uncover something. He dismissed the idea with the thought that if there was a problem, it was about to be solved.

*** *** *** ***

Max kept telling himself that being sent on a conference visit to Belfast was a good sign for his stagnant career. He was nursing a particular flat cappuccino watching the people rushing around. He was early for the flight. Not an unusual feat for most, but for Max this was a remarkable achievement. When he was born he was a week late, and to be honest, that was the beginning of an illustrious record of lateness. At university a seat at the back of the main lecture theatre that was closest to the door was designated Max's so as to cause the minimum of disturbance to the other students when he rolled in. He had even been late for his own wedding. An argument with the best man over the quickest route to the church led to them being stuck on the Chiswick flyover behind an accident. The two of them finally arrived on two bikes commandeered from the local post office. This time though it turned out he had little choice but to be early. Farmers had told him to check in at 6:30am for the 7:00am flight. He duly arrived at the Aer Lingus desk at around ten past seven assuming he'd catch the next one at 8:00am. The young lady behind the desk was amused at his apologies for being late.

"But you're two hours early," she had grinned.

"You're booked on the 9:00am flight."

It was then that he checked his ticket for the first time. It had meant that he could have breakfast. He walked over to the brightly lit café. He looked through the glass counter and although he resented paying six quid for a couple of overdone eggs and sausage and bacon that had sat under a heat lamp for an eternity he ordered and sat down. He would have plenty of fun people watching though. Of particular interest was the group of football supporters that looked as though they were about to fly off to Holland or somewhere. Their paraphernalia, hats and scarves etc. suggested their team was Arsenal, but it could have been any team playing out there and this bunch of lads would have been along for the ride. They were proud to be British, hence Union Jacks were sewn to virtually every item of clothing. On reflection, Britain may not at this particular moment in time be equally as proud of them. All were drunk to some level, and the most unfortunate was unconsciously laid over a pile of bags and rucksacks with a dopey grin on his face.

Unfortunate, because without consciousness his guard was down and two of his 'friends' (the term is used loosely here) were taking great pleasure in trying to wake him using just their flatulating talents. Max grinned as the larger of the two lost his footing and collapsed taking the other with him.

'Probably find he's a chartered surveyor or a lawyer in the week,' he mused. A security guard looked over briefly at the noise but thought better of any action. The other group of interest was four nuns. 'Always good for a laugh, nuns' Max thought. They were seated not far from the patriotic louts at the side of the cafe. Apart from the odd disapproving look and tut they didn't seem to react much to their surroundings.

'Couldn't do that,' he thought. 'Tough break being a nun. You can't have a bad day, can't swear, drink, get into fights, go bowling, have a decent vindaloo - tough break'. He realised his mind was wandering and checked his watch. Seven forty-five. He might as well go and check his bag in. It had been short notice for this conference and he'd had to go down to the dry cleaners at the last minute to pick up a suit.

'At least they'll have some decent whisky when I get there,' he smiled to himself as he handed his ticket and bag over.

"I'm afraid we've had to move your seat sir," said the green suited lady ever so politely.

"It's still inside the plane I trust," Max grinned but quickly realised it was too early in the morning to be flexing his wit.

"Er, yes, they've moved you forward to business class," she said with a smile.

"Well, I'll let it pass just this once," said Max in mock horror and strutted off as if he was in a really bad mood. This got a laugh from its target but a bunch of puzzled looks from the queuing passengers.

It was a small plane. Max disliked them normally as being the size he was, he never seemed to have enough leg room. But not today! Business Class. He glanced around the small section of perhaps twenty people. Four women, very well dressed and the rest men in suits and ties. He looked down at his choice of travelling attire. The jacket didn't really go with the trousers, the shirt was creased, no tie, and *'Oh bollocks,'* one navy sock and one black one.

'Well, if this plane crashes on a desert Isle then the girls won't be fighting over me,' he thought. *'Luckily there aren't many desert islands in the Irish sea,'* he added to the thought and grinned. The steward and the stewardess went through the life-jacket routine, no one paid attention. The moment they got the drinks trolley out though they became the central attraction. Max resisted the temptation to have a straight scotch, but had one with ginger ale instead. *'It's not like it's ten year old malt,'*

he thought as the steward placed the open can on his tray table. *'Oh balls,'* he thought, downed the scotch and offered the can of ginger ale to the bearded chap next to him. He declined, but very politely. So politely in fact that Max considered altering his long harboured opinions of red bearded people. *'Nah, still looks dodgy,'* he thought as he reached for the magazine in his seat front. 'Popular Yachting'. He placed it carefully back in its compartment and closed his eyes. It must have been a smooth flight because he only woke up as the wheels were touching the ground at the other end. He let out a huge yawn as the plane taxied and pulled to a stop. The passengers started to stumble off but the guy next to him was still fast asleep. *'Probably had a rough night,'* Max thought as he picked up his briefcase and walked out of the plane through the tunnel into the terminal. He had all afternoon before the conference opened that evening and he quite fancied a nice lunch and a gentle walk around the sights of Belfast. At the moment he need the loo. He spotted them just across the way and scuttled across. He checked himself in the mirror. He must have had his head lying to the left on the seat because his hair was all squashed on that side. A shower and spruce up at the hotel should do the trick. As he walked through the door he stepped into a scene of commotion. There were a lot of people shouting, and a few running toward the gate he had come from. He passed a couple of ambulancemen as he crossed to the cafe. Deciding to go for an Irish coffee (well when in Rome) he sat down in the corner and placed his order with a wave of the hand and some elaborate miming to the girl behind the counter.

"Excuse me, Sir". The voice came from a young looking security guard standing near to his table looking slightly nervous.

"Yes sunshine, what can I do you for?" Max replied looking up and finishing his coffee with a gulp.

"Would you mind coming with me, Sir," the young chap said slowly and quietly, almost as if he didn't want the other cafe customer to hear. *'Probably want me to point out a drunk guy on the plane that kept touching up the stewardess. There's always one.'* Max grinned. Max took one step out of the door and felt his briefcase snatched out of his hand and was thrown to the floor by a number of pairs of hands. On the way down the group of people in front of him was a blur, then a sharp bang on the ground. The last words he heard before the darkness closed in were

"Er, he's not moving much Sarge."

*** *** *** ***

The lights were bright. He closed his eyes again. His head hurt and he was lying down. He felt a hand on his shoulder and heard a female voice he didn't know. He tried to open his eyes again, still too bright. It didn't take a genius to work out that he was on a hospital bed of some sort, but how did he get there. His nose hurt too. He tried the eyes again - he could see a figure seated at the side of his bed.

"Welcome to the land of the living, Max." He knew the voice but couldn't place it. He slowly made out the face. Matthew Banks, his lawyer. He hadn't seen him in years. *'Must be getting some compensation for this accident,'* Max thought. Matthew looked solemn, but then he always did.

"So what do you think I'll get?" Max said cheerfully. Matthew nearly fell of his chair.

"Look Max, I don't know why you did this, well the news reports said way, but this is serious, you're looking at fifteen years."

"Er, what are you talking bout, I'm not getting any compensation for my fall?" Max was very, very puzzled.

"Reasonable force." Matthew said slowly.

"What, breaking my nose and knocking me unconscious?" Max snapped.

"You don't remember, do you?" Matthew said surprised. "Oh shit," he added.

"What's with the 'Oh shit', you never swear Matt," Max said sitting bolt upright in the bed.

"The guy next to you on the plane was a political activist for Sinn Fein," said Matthew.

"The IRA?" Max said stunned.

"Yes. He was poisoned and dead as a dodo by the end of the flight. The police had an anonymous tip off it was you and that you were armed - hence the 'reasonable force.'

"But that's crazy, why would I kill him, or anyone for that matter?" Max was struggling to find words.

"Max. I'm you're lawyer. If you tell me you didn't do it that's fine, but they found traces of the poison in your case".

"A plant," Max said blankly.

"And pictures of the man at your house, work, even diary entries pointing to it". Max swallowed hard, this had to be a very bad dream. "Look Max, if you didn't do it, and judging by the expression on you're face you didn't, then someone extremely clever had some reason to kill this person and they chose you for the fall guy."

(Matt watches too much American TV for his own good).

"But why me?" Max said still in shock.

"Who knows?" came the reply as Matthew took a buff coloured file out of his briefcase.

"They'll be charging you formally soon. The trial is set for the day after tomorrow. You made a lot of headlines and it looks like they want to get it over and done with as quickly as possible."

"What do I do?" Max asked blankly

"Well," Matthew hesitated

"Their evidence is clean cut but it is likely to go to a jury so I suppose there's always a chance. They do have some pretty damning video evidence which won't put the jury on your side."

"What?" Max asked puzzled once more.

"I've seen it. That anti-IRA march you took part in."

"But that was twenty years ago," Max pleaded.

"Yes, but you did thump a policeman."

"Oh yeah, after he belted me with his truncheon. I was never charged, he even bloody apologised!" Max said dismayed.

"I know, but the news footage of the march only shows the bit where you smacked him one," Matthew said slowly.

"Great" Max said burying his head in his hands.

"Look. I've spoken to the prosecution. They will go for a deal. It's not fantastic, but in the circumstances I have to admit I didn't expect anything."

Max sat up straight and took a deep breath.

"OK, what's the score?" he asked not wanting to know the answer.

"If you plead guilty they'll go with severe mental trauma and cut it down to manslaughter. Eight years in a secure institution. You'd probably be out in four or five."

"Oh just four or five years" Max shook his head.

"The alternative is they'll push hard for murder. On the strength of the evidence you will get life, with parole at about year nine."

"Either way I spend the next five years behind bars?"

"Yes. Look Max, if there was another way I'd find it, you know I would. I've been through their case. It's watertight. They've made it look meticulously planned and that the only thing that let you down was the tip off."

Max looked him square in the eyes.

"Not guilty," he said quietly and sternly.

"I was afraid of that," Matthew said forcing a smile, "which is why I drew these up." He reached for the file.

"Character statements from six pillars of society and my opening address," he said, placing them on the table next to Max who forced a smile.

"Oh, and I brought you these," he added pulling half a dozen packets of extra strong mints from his pocket.

"Don't eat them all at once," he said as he stood up and left the room. The click of the locks on the door left Max in silence and he stared at the white walls around him. He reached for the file and opened it. The first name was 'Jason Collinson', Mayor of Croydon. Max read the testimony slowly. It was glowing. He hadn't seen Jason for a couple of years, they'd sort of lost touch. As he read the words over again he smiled. Maybe he had a slim chance after all.

*** *** *** ***

"That's him," said James pointing to the television nestling on the bar. The younger man glanced over his shoulder and looked at the photograph displayed on the screen. It wasn't a particularly flattering photo. Max had been hung over when he had that passport picture done for a holiday in Spain. It was all messy hair and stubble. The volume on the television was turned low and he only made out the words

'....IRA.......peace process.....chilling precision.'

"James," said the other man quietly, "are you thinking we should kill him, maybe?"

James crossed his arms on the table in front of him and leaned forward.

"Maybe. But first I'm going to ask him why he did it."

*** *** *** ***

He had butterflies in his stomach and a sick feeling in his throat. His chest was heavy and his collar size shrunk three sizes too small. Max ran his fingers over the highly polished wood of the bench outside court number nine. There was a faint muttering of people coming and going along the corridors. Smiles were uncomfortably absent. Women and men in dark blue and grey suits looking so stern they could have been born that way talked to each other outside each set of doors. *'I'd like to get hold of the bastard that designed these corridor floors,'* he thought. Marble-like stone that meant a constant clicking of at least two or three pairs of high heels and the deeper thuds of the flat black conservative shoes that were the order of the day. His suit suddenly felt out of place. Was it too light? Would the judge think that he was a frivolous man? Max wished he'd worn that dark blue suit that had languished in the back of his wardrobe since his uncle's funeral two years before. Five minutes to go now. The time does go slower. Deep breaths, he should at least look calm. *'Now there's an organised man,* Max thought. *'He's got a dark blue suit, black briefcase, silver pens in the top pocket nestling next to the matching handkerchief. A wonderfully conforming paisley'.* He wished he hadn't worn that tie either. If this were the wild west then there would have been a dollar sign stamped on his forehead. This is not how it works in the films. Where was the bustling group of supporters for the condemned man, the snarling of teeth, cute stenographer and eerie classical score? His wife Jan kept popping back into his mind. He wasn't even allowed out of his cell to hold her. They had held hands through the bars. She had worried how suspiciously fast the case had come to court. She told him everything was going to be all right but bar a miracle this would be a short sharp trip to the Isle of Wight. The two guards next to him on the bench suddenly stirred and lifting him up via the cuffs they walked Max to the door. The time they had been sitting there they had been like gargoyles. Going through the two fairly plain wooden doors could not have led to a more stirring scene. The courtroom erupted and the public gallery seemed awash with angry faces and placards. As he lifted his eyes they met those of a young lady who was screaming abuse. He managed to make out the words 'Scum' and 'Peace wrecker' from the taunts. One of the officials quickly ordered the court to be cleared and Max could see people being dragged out by the hordes of policeman present. Within a minute the public gallery was empty apart from a group of news hounds eagerly scribbling away at their pads. As Max was shown to his seat still connected to the two officers he looked over at the prosecutor's table. Dark suit, paisley ensemble - Mr.Organised.

'*Oh Shit,*' thought Max. Not for the first time that day.

From where he sat Max was probably ten yards from the jury that had been selected to seal his fate. As he cast his eyes over the two rows of six he wished he could change places with any of them. There were four women and eight men (though one of the latter could have passed for one of the former judging by what he was wearing). They all seemed eager to avoid eye contact with him; understandable in the circumstances. Max's two escorts, still handcuffed to him, look bored already.

'*Not much scope for job satisfaction,*' thought Max looking at the two of them.

"Do you mind if I have a mint?" Max whispered to 'Leftie,' as he had dubbed the officer attached to his left arm. The officer forced a smile and reached into Max's top pocket to retrieve yet another new packet of mints. That was the third that morning. They'd seen him go through a whole packet in his cell when they went to get him and another on the way here.

'*Mmm, taste a bit off,*' Max thought as he crunched away. 'Rightie' had decided to go for a mint as well and also wondered why they tasted peculiar. As the officer fell forward his head just missed the bench in front of him. Max was a little taller and the whole court turned as the thud of skull against wood rang out.

It was dark and wet and the little bit of light there was seemed to be fighting a losing battle. By squinting the two men could make out the open hatch above them. One of them walked directly below it and looked up. About ten feet above him the dim light of the laundry room was visible.

"Are you sure they'll bring him here?" he asked as he turned around.

"Put it this way, I wouldn't want to be standing where you are now when they do," came the reply.

Most stretchers are designed for one individual. On this occasion there were two bodies squashed in a haphazard way still connected to a third who was in turn wedged at the back of the ambulance. The doctor and nurse made it a very cosy five as the driver wound round another corner. The nurse was alternating between the two horizontally aligned men checking they were still alive while the doctor frantically examined the remains of the packet of mints. The other conscious passenger was anxiously searching his brain for a plausible explanation as to how a prisoner in his charge and his colleague had been poisoned. His position had been further embarrassed by the sudden disappearance of the man with the keys to the handcuffs (an officer with quite sever bladder problems who was holed up in the loo at the time of the two men's collapse). His radio crackled into life.

"Romeo Victor this is Alpha One. Do you read?"

"Roger Alpha One," he replied quickly.

"The officer with the keys to the cuffs is at the emergency doors of the hospital, please inform the ambulance crew."

"Roger Alpha One," he said and looked at the doctor who nodded that he'd overheard.

The receiving crew at the hospital had been told to expect two cases of poisoning. They were mildly curious as to why a police officer (well he had to be a type of copper as he appeared to be desperately trying not to look like one) with a bunch of keys was waiting with them.

"Bet you don't get this sort of excitement down at St. Judes," Alex grinned to the new boy Simon who'd been transferred over from there the day before.

"Oh sometimes," he smiled, "Don't forgot we're just down the road from the Milwall football ground. Things can get a little racy of a Saturday afternoon."

"I can't find anything yet," said the doctor in a frustrated tone.

'I wonder what I'll wear for Jimmy's work do,' thought the nurse as she checked their pulses once more.

"Still alive and sort of kicking," she said as they turned through the gates of the hospital and screeched to a halt outside the doors to emergency.

"Do you think they'll be long?" asked the young lad in the dim tunnel. He was sitting on the trolley and watching the drops falling from the ceiling.

"I shouldn't think so," said James as he looked at his watch. By his calculations their package should fall from above in the next five minutes.

The man with the keys lunged through the ambulance doors and unlocked the handcuffs. He sneered at the officer still pinned to the back wall and leapt back out to give the attendants a hand.

"I've got this one," Simon shouted yanking the slightly larger of the two men onto a stretcher. Alex reached for the other and spun around to find that Simon was already speeding halfway down the corridor.

The scene outside the hospital doors was bedlam. Two dozen police officers trying to keep a mass of journalists at bay. Puzzled patients looked on as a succession of policemen scuttled down the corridors heading for the emergency room. Simon rounded the next corner and stopped the trolley in front of the utility room door. He turned around and braced himself. The door opened, the trolley was pulled in and after a hollow thumping noise Simon slumped to the ground and was dragged inside. A few seconds after the door clicked shut Matthew rounded the corner closely followed by a group of policeman and officials and flew down toward the emergency room.

There was no lock on the inside of the utility room so he had to be quick. The man on the trolley was quite a size so he manoeuvred as close as he could to the opening of the laundry chute and pushed him in feet first. It was quite a squeeze. He swore under his breath as he wedged his shoulder against the motionless lump and pushed.

The doctors in the emergency room watched calmly as the doors flung open and Alex flew in. They transferred the officer to the operating table and attached a host of tubes.

"And the other one?" enquired the taller of the two doctors in a sharp voice that didn't sound at all interested. A number of hovering faces turned and scanned the room which wouldn't have concealed a small sausage dog let alone an eighteen stone man on a trolley.

The body was stuck halfway down the chute. The person who pushed it there was blissfully unaware of this until he followed it and felt a bump as his feet hit its head and dislodged it. The makeshift ramp in the laundry room did its job though as the body rumbled down and slid straight down the hatch into the sewer piping. Arriving moments later, the man leapt off the ramp, dismantled it and followed down the piping shutting the cover as he went. The thump was slightly louder than the splash (but it was a close call) as Max's body landed in the sewer. He was about to take his second trolley ride of the day but sadly he wasn't going to remember this one either.

By the time the three plain clothed officers reached the laundry room, and had put two and two together (more cynical commentators here would suggest that for plain clothed policemen this was an achievement in itself) the body on the trolley had covered a few hundred metres through the sewer, been lifted out through a manhole in a back street and dumped under a blanket in the back of a plain white transit van. Another five minutes and the van was on the south circular. Another ten and it had become a blue Renault.

Max had always been sceptical that you could tell a lot about a person from their eyes, but had never been in a situation in which to put it to the test, until now. The three men that he could see in the back of the van were all wearing masks and looking into their eyes he saw nothing but harsh concentration. It is amazing how in all the big-budget thrillers churned out by Hollywood no one has ever mentioned that being scared witless and having adrenaline running rampant through your veins in fact enhances your senses tenfold. At that particular moment, with the feel of cold steel against his temple, Max's sense of smell was equal to that of a blind man. Unfortunately, the position of the pistol meant the revealed armpit of one of his captors - the sweatiest of the bunch. As his eyes plunged into darkness from a painful thud against the aforementioned temple Max made a mental note. *'Add to the important to remember list; If you encounter a crazed paramilitary with a personal hygiene problem, keep it to yourself...........'*

'A chair. A room. Four walls. A table. Body tied to the chair. Man coming through the door with a cloth pad, pushing it over my mouth. Darkness......'

Max was beginning to get annoyed with the process of regaining consciousness. This time the effects of the chloroform had given him a splitting headache much like a hangover. He was in the back of a van again. The first thing he noticed was that he was breathing through his nose. This was directly attributable to the thick piece of tape that had been wound across his mouth. His hands were tied behind his back too. There were two men in the back of the van with him and Max could hear the third, the driver, talking loudly in the front. The van was moving. The younger lad he recognised from the previous van ride. The other was different. Conversation was out, so Max tried to examine his surroundings. It was a different van from the last, smaller and more compact. It had no sliding door and a single hatch door at the back. The two men both had stern expressions on their faces and pistols on their laps. The younger one realised that Max had woken up and grinned at him. He then tapped the butt of his pistol against the palm of his left hand. Max looked over at the other man who was larger and stockier. His clothes were rougher and almost exclusively denim.

"What do you think you're looking at scum?" he sneered at Max and gave him a hard punch to the ribs. Max tried to cough which was impossible with his mouth taped up. The result was a lot of heavy breathing through his nose and his eyes began to water. For the first time in his life Max wondered whether he'd be better off dead. People sometimes say it but it takes a lot to make you actually think it. He thought fate had been listening when he felt the impact of the lorry which threw him onto the floor. He heard some shouting before another bang as the van bounced off the central reservation onto its side and was pinned there by the lorry. He was bounced around like a rag doll. A montage of blurred images that he later suspected had been his life flashed before his eyes and then nothing but green. He squinted. They had stopped moving. He heard more shouting and out of the corner of his eye he could see the back door being forced open. The younger lad was being carried out covered in blood. Max realised the green colour in front of him was the shirt of the other man who was slumped in front of him. He managed to get onto his knees and shuffled out of the back door and into the sunshine. The scene was chaos. About a dozen cars had been going too fast to avoid the lorry and were across the carriageway at all angles. Many others had pulled up and were helping people out of their cars. The screams of a man with a broken leg diverted most of the helpers' attention to his red estate car which was wedged underneath the side of the lorry. Max managed to slip into the ditch in between the carriageways unnoticed and slowly made his way along it. After fifty yards he got off his knees and stood up cautiously. The traffic was backing up now and he could hear sirens coming closer. Running with your hands behind your back is somewhat of an art form but Max managed to make it across the other carriageway and into the woods boarding the motorway. His progress through the trees and bushes was more cautious after he fell flat on his face the second time. He need not have panicked as the other three from the van were in a pretty bad state and were being attended to by a couple of ambulance crews. After stumbling for half an hour he came to the edge of the wood which met the back of a small industrial estate. He slowly approached a large brown building. Tired, aching and surprisingly hungry Max staggered in through the warehouse door of a furniture importers. The store man could scarcely believe his eyes as Max slumped into a chair outside his office. A cut over Max's left eyebrow had left a streak of dried blood down his face and he looked very worse for wear. The store man shouted to the secretary for the first aid kit and the two of them slowly removed the tape from Max's mouth. After spluttering for a while he forced a smile.

"What the hell happened to you?" asked the store man as he cleaned the cut carefully with a damp pad of cotton wool.

Within two hours of the police's arrival at the scene of the motorway pile up the phone in Anders' hotel room rang and his contact at New Scotland Yard gave him the location. The firearms in the back of the van had been traced to an IRA cell that was operating on the mainland. After a half dozen calls Anders and Easton vacated their rooms, settled the accounts with cash and made their way to the car parked across the street. At the same time a dozen office workers in the Oxford area took an unexpected afternoon off.

The cup of tea and half a packet of digestive biscuits had put Max in a better frame of mind. He wasn't sure the two that had just cleaned him up had believed his story and he was a little worried that they had reached for the phone to call the police the moment he had stepped out of the door. He wasn't going to take any chances and as soon as he was around the corner he climbed over a fence and headed off through a field of deep grass at a quick pace. He had no cause for alarm as the store man was currently filling the secretary in on a similar incident in his family when his cousin had been caught by his wife with his next door neighbour. He'd got away with a broken nose and a couple of black eyes. This guy had been less lucky. Fancy torching his car and dumping him in the woods. Relatives could be so vindictive.

***   ***   ***   ***

The slow monotonous beep of the machines would have cured even the most committed insomniac. The man in front of her was a shadow of the man that she had stood by for thirty years. The room was cold to the eye despite the obvious attempts to create a sense of comfort. The promises of the doctors rang hollow in her mind. Was he going to get better? Her heart held out hope but her mind had long given up. Countless operations had chipped away at her faith in him regaining consciousness and coming home once more.

***   ***   ***   ***

The smoke was beginning to get to Peter. If he could choose a place to be on a Sunday afternoon this would not be it. The pub was large and this was the busier bar - the 'lounge bar'. Most of the clientele were older country types but there were two or three groups of younger people and these were the focus of his attention. If the rumours were true and he could get more information then maybe he could finally get shot of the tin-pot local paper and get touted by one of the nationals. The 'Wessex Warbler' had never carried a story as strong as this and it was half written already. 'Satanic Sacrifices in the Home Counties'. He had plenty of background. Now if he could get an interview with a worshipper, or get himself invited to a sacrifice... This last thought lifted his spirits considerably and he sipped his pint and moved over to a stool at the bar. Unbeknown to him the group next to him were pig farmers.

"..........and that'll mean we get two to slaughter in one go," said the man in the Argyle sweater and green boots. Peter's ears pricked up and he listened more intently.

"But you'll have to be careful - you know how the blood gets everywhere," the other man warned and motioned with his arms

'This is great!' Peter thought and leaned yet closer. *'The tip off was right, and they seem so brazen about it all.'*

Unfortunately the stool he was sitting on was not designed for leaning and before he could do anything Peter felt himself falling backwards. Its quite amazing how far three quarters of a pint of lager can travel with the slightest provocation. Before Peter had even hit the floor most of the liquid had passed over the saloon bar doors and slammed into the back of a large man dressed in leather bikers gear. As he hit the floor, the glass hit the large man in the back of the head. Peter's fall had gone unnoticed in the noise of the lounge bar but the commotion in the next bar was considerable. The leather, and now beer clad, biker after a brief dizzy moment had rounded on a well dressed man standing next to the saloon doors. He had been laughing at something his friend had just said and was waiting for his next drink from another mate at the bar. To the wounded man the laughter and empty hands were more than enough evidence and he shook his fists and began pushing the man into the wall. The smaller man rallied and with two swift jabs he caught the heavier man full on the chin putting him swiftly onto his backside. The rest of the bar had begun cheering as the biker got clumsily to his feet, shook his head and charged at the man again.

Meanwhile Peter was on all fours moving quickly through the maze of feet in the bar. He could see a door and was going to get to it as quickly as possible. He was almost there when a lady decided to change position on her chair and move her stilettoed feet. Peter saw them coming and closed his eyes and braced himself. Nothing. He opened his eyes at a squint and saw the heel neatly placed between his finger and thumb. A bead of sweat glistened on his brow as he gently removed his hand. A few more shuffles and he was through the doors. He'd been on his knees for so long it didn't occur to him to stand up and he aimed for the next door he could see. He found himself inside a telephone booth and this prompted him to stand up. He could hear the rumpus going on in the bar but it was fairly faint. He picked up the receiver quickly and pretended to be listening to someone on the other end. There was someone in the booth next to him and instinctively he tried to make out what the man was saying.

"Yes it is important, I've already said that......yes I'll hold." The man sounded agitated. It didn't sound too interesting but Peter didn't fancy going back into the bar just now.

"Yes, I want to speak to Kathy. It is a matter of life and death."

'Hmmm, that sounds better,' Peter thought.

There was a brief silence then the man continued.

"Hello Kathy? Yes, yes its me.... Yes, I'm fine.... No I can't, they'd find me if I said...I just wanted to say I was OK and alive. Is everything ok there?.......I thought they might have……What men took what files?….Which patients?…Mr Verdkyll!… I knew it!…..I'd better go…..I'll call again soon, please tell my wife I'm OK, they've probably tapped my home phone...."

'Sod sacrifices,' Peter thought *'This guy's on the run from someone, don't know who but I'm sure as hell going to find out.'*

He heard the receiver go down in the next booth and waited until he heard the adjoining door open. It was then that he saw him. The same man as on the 10 o'clock news the night before. Max something or other - hit man who had broken free.

'Wow what a story!' he thought as he slipped out of the booth and the side door of the pub following the big man's footsteps.

Two men left the lounge bar half a minute later. They headed down the same lane as they left the pub. Peter had seen him go down this alley but it was long and deserted.

'Surely he couldn't have reached the other end so quickly,' he thought.

His eyes nearly popped out of his head as a large hand shot out of a gap in the fence and grabbed his throat. Within a second a gate opened wide and Peter was pulled inside and the gate closed quickly. He saw the face close up now. It was rounder than it looked on the telly but the dark hair and dark eyes were unmistakable. The man motioned to him to be quiet and Peter strained his eyes toward the fence. He could hear footsteps moving past and within a minute the grip around his neck was released.

"You're not going to kill me?" he stammered.

"Hell no," Max said, "but they might," he added motioning to the alleyway.

"I think they think you're with me," he smiled.

Peter considered this for a moment. "You're Max Jones aren't you?"

"Yes," Max replied, "And you are?" he asked sarcastically.

"Pete, but who are they?" Peter asked, forever the reporter despite the fact he was moments from mortal danger.

"The IRA I assume - well they seemed pretty annoyed I managed to get free."

"The IRA?" Peter said with genuine surprise. "Did they break you out?" he asked

"Yep, it was just as much a shock for me too," Max whispered.

"Did you kill that guy then - the one on the news?" Peter couldn't believe he was having a whispered conversation with an alleged hit-man, down an alley.

"No, I was set up," Max replied.

"I knew it!" Peter whispered with an air of satisfaction.

"I'm the only one in the office that bet on you being innocent," he added smugly.

"I'm touched," said Max and still with sarcasm. "Now look. You'd better get your ass out of here or you'll end up six feet under, which is probably where I'll be before the day is out..."

Before Max could finish they heard a man shouting from the other end of the alley. Max bolted and climbed over the wall a few feet behind them. Without thinking Peter followed. His feet landed with a thump, which he felt mostly in his knees. He saw the large man disappear around the corner of some houses and with the excitement of a kid on Xmas morning he ran after him.

If he were to be chased by the IRA again Max would probably not choose a motorcycle as his getaway vehicle. However, the petrol station beckoned and the gleaming Honda, which had thoughtfully just been filled by its owner, was sitting there with the keys in it. Peter stopped dead as Max leapt on.

"You surely don't intend on taking that," he blurted out but before Max could answer a bullet rattled the row of oil-cans next to the pump. Despite being half his size Peter seemed to get his hands all the way around Max's waist in an instant and the engine roared into life. The bike wobbled left and right for the first 100 yards or so as Max got used to the controls again. It had been a good ten years since he'd ridden a bike as a motorcycle courier. There was that kick again! The rush of wind and weaving around the tight corners of the little village Max was in his element. His face broke into a broad grin, in complete contrast to Peter whose first time on the back of 750cc of Japanese steel gave him the look of person reaching the highest peak of a roller coaster. The two figures had switched their feet for a somewhat faster Rover. A few miles out of the village on a straight piece of road Max motioned to Peter to pass him the spare helmet. He could have assumed this was to protect his face from the wind, but it had more to do with drowning out Peters cries and moans. An inquisitive herd of cows watched closely as the bike followed now by the car sped past a small farm. Max was having far too much fun to pay too much attention to the danger behind. Thoughtfully though they gave him the odd reminder of the small coned cylindrical type. Max felt Peter's grip tighten considerably and his right leg drop away. He'd gone quiet too. He'd been hit. As abruptly as it had begun the fun-ride stopped. Max focused his attention on the predicament. How was he going to lose the car? Should he get off the main roads where the police would surely be looking for the stolen bike very soon? He also needed to find a doctor for Peter. The next road sign triggered something in his mind and he opened up the bike even further. As soon as the speed increased it was slammed down by the back of a 16 wheeler blocking the road ahead. Go around on a blind corner or get shot - easy choice - he threw the bike out into the middle of the road. *'Isn't that just great,'* Max thought as the oncoming truck rounded the corner. "Breathe in!" he screamed into his helmet - plenty of room - OK, so both of the mirrors had been torn off the bike in the process but at least the car couldn't follow. Hard left, then right, left again. He took random turns for perhaps ten minutes. Max pushed the bike until his heart finally stopped racing. *'Well if they're still with us they deserve to get us,'* Max thought as he pulled in behind a farm building. He was relieved to hear only the cackling of a couple of chickens as he turned off the engine. Removing his helmet he looked back at his passenger. "Pete you OK?" - judging by the expression on his face that was a pretty dumb question. Peter's leg was bleeding as he gingerly got off the bike. He managed a small grin as Max slapped him gently on the back. *'I'm going to die,'* Peter thought as he looked at Max. *'if this bloody bullet doesn't kill me his driving will'.*

"I've been better," he muttered.

"OK I'm sorry, but I know someone who'll sort this out for us," said Max

"What a doctor?" Peter replied surprised.

"Sort of," Max paused "He used to be, he's a vet now."

"Oh great, just wheel me in next to Flossy, Daisy and Lassie," Peter groaned.

"It'll be fine," Max said reassuringly. " I met him at a piss up at a Union conference, he lives about forty miles North of here in Tilverton".

After washing the wound under a tap inside the barn and covering it with a clean handkerchief Max helped Peter back onto the bike and slowly edged down the small lanes. It had now begun to get dark and Max decided to keep the bike for it was easier to hide than a car, and besides, he didn't know how to hot-wire a car. The journey to Tilverton was slow but without incidence and they soon pulled up by the phonebox at the edge of town.

"Hello, 45728." the voice was deep and friendly

"Hello Angus, its Max.....Bournemouth last year, remember?"

"Max you old sod, of course I remember! It's not every day I get arrested for indecent exposure."

"Ah yes, the midnight swim, well we had had a few beers," Max grinned

"It's great to hear from you, but aren't you supposed to be a wanted dangerous criminal on the run?"

"What do you think," Max laughed, "me, a hit-man?"

"Of course not, only kidding. Is there anything I can do to help?"

"Well actually, a cup of tea would go down a treat. We're in the phonebox opposite the clock tower. You did say that if I was ever in the area."

"Great! Harbouring escapees happens to be one of my favourite pastimes - follow the road out of town up the hill and take the second left - we're the first place on the right."

"Thanks mate," Max said and put the receiver down gently with a heavy sigh. He looked out at Peter who was propping up his head with his hands. *'He's a good lad,'* thought Max. His jeans were torn in a number of places and where they weren't bloody they were covered in mud.

"Hey Pete," he called over, "fancy a nice cup of tea?" he said smiling.

"If there's a brandy in it," came the weary reply.

Within five minutes they had pulled up in front of a small cottage to be met by a goat that was wandering around the front garden. The flicker of an open fire reached them through a porthole window next to the front door. Max reached for the large brass knocker and gave a series of thumps. Almost immediately the door opened and was filled by a tall bearded man sporting a huge grin

"Max, I heard you come up the lane. What are you riding? Sounds like a tank."

'His handshake is as strong as ever,' Max thought as he retrieved his hand from the big man's grip.

"Angus, I've got someone with me. Pete this is Angus. Angus, Pete. He's picked up a bit of a scratch, do you mind taking a look at him?" Max asked as they walked through into the hallway.

"Sure, I'll get Anne to sort out my bag," Angus smiled.

"This is Pete," Max announced as he ushered the limping Peter into the warm lounge. Anne emerged smiling and carrying a large black bag. She was very different to her husband, small and pretty, her dark brown wavy hair touching her shoulders. Strong arms though. Angus towered over even Max although his size was softened by the thick brown beard hanging below his messy mousy hair. The thick grey woolly jumper and cords made him look almost cuddly, which is an achievement for a man of 6'4".

"So 'e fall of the bike then?" enquired the big man as he showed Peter to the small sofa in the corner of the room. Max held back his reply as Angus looked at the outstretched leg. His smile suddenly left his face. "Max, for god's sake he's got a bullet in his thigh!" he frowned as he turned round to Max who was perched on the edge of an armchair.

74

"I suppose you wouldn't believe that it was from a freak duck hunting accident?" Max offered lamely.

"What do you think, and before you answer that I don't think I really want to know," Angus sighed reaching inside his bag.

"I suppose not, but can you fix him?"

"I can't promise he'll be able to enter the 'Miss Lovely Legs' pageant this year but the bullet is fairly accessible. I think it must have hit something else first as its not too deep. I had a similar wound with the Jones' mare and a pebble last week."

"Oh great," Peter groaned softly.

"Here's your tea young man," Anne smiled as she handed him a large cream coloured mug.

Peter drank the tea and watched as Max and Angus chatted with great animation and frequent bouts of laughter recalling their exploits in Bournemouth. He'd begun to like this big guy Max Jones. He could come across a bit brash, and OK he was really stubborn, and I suppose he could do with a few evening classes at charm school, but deep down he was an OK guy. There was no way he was a killer. The goings on at the hospital did reek of something and he was sure that it was all linked with Max being set up. It was very well done, but the question was, by whom. It was going to be a fantastic story he thought. Mmm, nice cup of tea.

"So, where's the anaesthetic," Peter piped up.

"You've just drunk it," Max laughed and Peter joined in as he felt his eyelids go heavy and the room slowly drift into darkness.

*** *** *** ***

Peter awoke to the sound of a cow mooing. It seemed pretty loud and as he squinted and put on his glasses he turned his head toward the window.

"MOOOOO..." It was definitely a cow and a large one at that. It was standing outside the window with its head through the opening and approximately six inches from his face. Its focus appeared to be the vase of fresh flowers on the bedside table.

'Where on earth am I?' Peter thought as he looked around the small room. It was very cosy. A lot of floral designs with everything matching, from the curtains to the tablecloth. He wasn't unduly worried as it looked like a nice enough place. The cow and lack of noise suggested he was somewhere in the countryside. It took a few more moments before the previous day's events came flooding back to him. The dull numbness of his left leg signalled his complete return to consciousness. He took a deep breath - clean air!

'This is a great story,' he thought. He was on the run with one of the most notorious criminals of the past few years, been chased by the IRA and shot into the bargain. No more 'Local fisherman catches Wellington boot' stories - no more standing in the pouring rain on a Sunday afternoon watching Melchester Junior 11 get hammered by another equally obscure team of young louts. The sun was out and the smell of a country morning fuelled Peter's appetite for adventure. The cow was now more than half way through the flowers and paying him little attention. He'd lived near the countryside all his life and had almost become oblivious to its beauty. His visits to farms had, in the majority of cases resulted in getting covered in mud and/or having abuse thrown at him. Farmers, like most people have an almost in-built dislike for journalists. He was about to attempt to leap out of bed when the door opened and a tray appeared in the gap. At first the steam from a pot of tea obscured the face of the person holding the tray, but nevertheless the cow instinctively knew who it was and hastily withdrew its head.

"Good morning young man," said Anne smiling.

"Hello," replied Peter glad to see the friendly face almost as much as the huge breakfast on the tray. This was, in all possible definitions a 'full' English breakfast.

"You're quite a lucky chap you know," Anne grinned as she laid the tray across his lap.

"It's not common around here to have received a bullet and been around the next morning," her grin turned to a laugh and Peter joined in.

"Thanks for the hospitality," Peter said thinking it sounded naff but not really knowing what to say.

"Oh, that's OK. Angus does have some unusual friends I'll give him that. Max is a great fella though, heart of gold," she said as she left the room. This suggested he should eat, and he wasn't going to argue. He was starving and got stuck in.

The path ran alongside the hedgerow that separated the cornfields from the grazing land. It wasn't wide enough for two people and as Angus walked through the knee deep grass in his boots they glistened with the morning dew.

"What now?" he asked.

Max was walking slowly with his hands in his pockets and a thoughtful expression on his face.

"To be honest, I'm not altogether sure. I know I'm the subject of an elaborate set-up, I have very little proof and virtually no expertise with which to validate the little I have. Both the police and the IRA are looking for me and I have already got one person shot." At this last sentence he paused and Angus quickly added,

"Yes, but Peter came with you voluntarily remember," he said firmly

" I suppose so," Max agreed but that didn't detract much from the fact that it had still been his fault.

"I need to find someone with knowledge in the neural area. Maybe they could piece together what these people were up to," Max said as he started walking again. They were now half way down the narrow path which lead to what could be loosely described as a barn of some sort.

"If you need to stay a while, the offer's open," said Angus putting his arm on Max's shoulder.

"The lad ought to rest a couple of days. It was only a little nick but he could do with taking it easy," he added. Somewhere back toward the cottage a cock crowed loudly prompting both men to turn around just in time to see Anne emerge from the house waving frantically what looked like a newspaper.

They had made second page news. The rundown of the chase down country lanes, the stolen bike and Max's 'kidnap' of an unknown hostage would probably have made it to the front page except another Royal crisis had broken overnight and the papers were all jostling for position with different 'Exclusives'. The Telegraph carried the headline 'One is not amused' next to a picture of the queen they'd managed to dig up where she had a frown on her face. Max read their story intently. Despite containing a surprising amount of accurate facts it has been glamorised considerably. He was flattered at being described as an 'expert' biker and Peter was annoyed at being labelled 'anonymous'. The one good thing was that the paper suggested that he had fled west into Avon, probably to Bristol or Gloucester and that area was being monitored heavily by the police. That put him a good 150 miles away from scrutiny.

*** *** *** ***

This was embarrassing. Easton knew it. Anders knew it. The latter was on the phone in a small hotel in Berkshire. The call was transatlantic and the person on the other end was not amused. Apart from standing at a phone booth in the pouring rain on a biting Brooklyn morning, he was getting little out of a stubborn Anders as to why things were not going to plan.

"He'll be dead within a week," Anders snarled and put down the receiver. He was embarrassed more than he had ever been in his career. The saga had dragged on for months now. He would have put a bullet in the guy's head long ago but the agency decided on this IRA thing. Very messy. It had run perfectly but with such an unpredictable group as the IRA they should have been more careful. Now they had the man at the centre of it all running loose around the countryside. At least the British had assumed the IRA had been behind the previous day's chase. That was how it must stay. He was sure that Max didn't know what the hell was going on. Heck, even they didn't know the half of it. As far as the rest of the world was concerned this Max character was going to leave this earth at the hands of avenging IRA gunmen. It would have to be soon though, as the longer it went on the more loose ends there would be to tied up, and he was already bored with England.

**** **** **** ****

In the four days that Max and Peter stayed at the farmhouse the focus of the media remained strong. Each day every available newspaper was bought from the village store by Angus, much to the bemusement of the shop's grey-haired owner. Speculation was rife as to Peter's identity, and names of missing persons from all corners of the country entered and left the fray with quick succession. Various theories as to why the IRA had not killed Max outright were being bandied about, from the amusing to the ridiculous. One paper had on the Monday run the idea that the IRA wanted to find the people behind Max as they felt he was just a pawn in some large international conspiracy. This was quickly forgotten the following day when Scotland Yard released a statement.

"It has been made known by a source within the IRA that abduction of Max Jones was not sanctioned by the main leaders but carried out by a hard-line faction whose sole purpose was to avenge the murder for which he was being tried."

The media and the British public seemed to take this as almost read. Most sources now reported that Max had left the country and he had even been spotted in Geneva of all places. Max smiled at the thought of being in Switzerland.

'A bit wide of the mark,' he thought as he sipped a steaming mug of cocoa. Peter sat opposite him in a fireside chair with his cheeks a healthy glow from sitting so close to the open fire. He was cutting more pieces from the day's papers and scribbling notes on them. He finished with the scissors and struck up a conversation.

"Where are we off to then," his voice sounded light as ever and his strength had definitely returned.

"I am off to try and clear my name," came Max's stern reply.

"I thought you might try that," replied Peter as if rehearsed. He continued in a confident tone.

"Firstly you need help, especially in getting your side of the story across."

"Yeah but…,"Max tried to argue but Peter was on a roll.

"And secondly, I know where you've been, what you have done and where you're likely to go."

"You mean you would turn me in?" Max said sounding hurt. This didn't deter his young friend who grinned and added, "The story gets written Max - as soon as we part company."

Max shrugged and sat back in his chair. He admired this lad and although it was a cliché he reminded him of a certain stubborn lad he once was. The major plus point was that he fervently believed in Max's innocence. He was a good partner to have, even if the sole benefit was to keep Max sane.

"Thanks for the choice," Max said quietly as he stood up and went to the kitchen. He looked out of the window at a clear starry sky. His wife would be watching the stars too. He could picture her on the balcony at the back of the house - sitting there in dressing gown and quilt and the dulcet tones of Smokey Robinson filtering through from the lounge. He'd left messages at her work every day of his recent freedom. He knew to talk to her was too risky - who knows who would be listening. He sighed as he poured another steaming cup of cocoa into a mug.

"OK," he said slowly as he returned to the living room.

"This is for your ears only, I'm not going to tell Angus and Anne which way we are going." Peter nodded and perched on the edge of his seat.

"There is a lecturer at Southampton University, a neurology expert . He owes a mate of mine a favour and I think he'll help."

"How?" Peter's pen was poised and Max had his complete attention.

"I need him to find a reason why those behind the research are so anxious to keep the tests they are doing on people's brain tissue quiet, and why they were taking the tissue while they were still living."

"You mean they were taking parts of people's brains while they were still living?" Peter said with a look of horror and disgust on his face.

"Uh huh, well sort of. All of the patients I can remember, except the last two, had life threatening illnesses and were being kept on life support systems," Max replied.

"And the last two?" Peter was fascinated and his pen was working overtime.

" They had come in with neural problems, but not necessarily fatal. They were obviously getting desperate."

Peter opened his mouth to speak but paused and seemed to be thinking.

"Any proof?" he asked

"Some," Max sighed, "but it's of no use until I find out what research they would have been doing. It's secret enough to kill for."

"Could it be cancer or HIV or something like that?" Peter suggested.

"I suppose so, but we're scratching around in the dark. Hopefully this guy can give me a better idea," Max smiled.

"And then?"

"Then we take another look at my proof to see how much it's really worth."

The additional time spent at Angus and Anne's had been put to good use. The bike had been painted and a number plate from an old cycle and sidecar switched onto it. Max had cut his hair short and dyed it jet black and both he and Peter had a complete change of clothes. This latter point was achieved with some difficulty as although Angus and Max were roughly the same size, Peter was much smaller. He was kitted out in a wool sweater that had shrunk in the wash and some of Anne's jogging bottoms. They also had matching raincoats. As they sat on the bike in the misty morning sun, Angus smiled and shook both of their hands in turn. *'They won't win any fashion prizes,'* he thought.

"I'd never recognise you," he said trying to keep a straight face.

"Its not really you I'm worried about," laughed Max. He turned the key and the bike kicked into life and purred like an oversized kitten. They had exchanged helmets and Peter was now wearing a blue one and Max the red. They both shook violently as Max guided the bike down the lane. It was 5am. They would be well on their way to Southampton before anyone was on the roads. Had they not had their helmets on they may have heard the flock of sheep bleating as they pulled onto the main road. Twenty miles further on, had they been looking for it, they may have seen a green four door Jaguar pull out of a small lane and take the same A40 turning they made. It was going to be "an overcast of day with afternoon showers," well at least according to Radio 4 and that was good enough for Max. Sure enough, after they had completed over half of their journey and they had found the M3 it began to drizzle. Max decided to stop off at a motorway service station for a quick break.

The service station was busy and Max and Peter finally found a table in the corner of the packed café. Max had swapped his helmet for a peaked cap and Peter smiled as they sat watching the hustle and bustle.

"You look more like James Herriot every day you know," Peter smirked.

"That's rich coming from a person with the colour co-ordination of a blind chameleon," Max replied with a large grin on his face. This isn't going to be as bad as I thought Max mused as he gulped down the steaming coffee.

'Only 60 miles to Southampton, we should be there by 11,' he thought.

"I've never actually seen one of these places busy," Peter piped up.

"Well you haven't lived then," Max said sarcastically.

"Its great for people watching though don't you think?" Peter added

"Suppose so," Max agreed. He was too busy thinking to chat, but Peter seemed to be in the mood to talk so he made an effort.

"I see what you mean. Take that guy over there by the counter. Yeah, the tall one. Its raining, dim and dull and he's wearing sunglasses indoors."

"Hey, maybe he's got eyesight problems?" Peter suggested

"Nah, more like social problems. He looks like a raincoat pervert."

"OK, Mr Expert, how about the man at the table in the corner. He looks more normal -tell me about him," Peter smiled.

"Ah yes. Young, short black hair and a really dull suit. I reckon he's 26 if he's a day and a sales rep."

"What does he sell?" asked Peter who was enjoying the game.

"Shower curtains and sometimes watches."

"What out of a suitcase!" Peter laughed.

"Oh yeah, and his name's Kevin."

"OK, the girl at the next table from him?"

"Blonde, 22. Training to be a scuba diving instructor."

"Definitely," Peter laughed again.

"OK, now a really tough one. The two badly dressed guys sitting at this table."

The voice was deep and threatening and accompanied by the barrel of a gun firmly pressed between Max's shoulder blades.

"That's a toughie," Max coughed.

"Max Jones and Pete Smalt, two smartasses currently training to be corpses," Anders said quietly. Peter looked anxiously over at Max.

"It's the dopey one with the sunglasses," he said through clenched teeth.

"Shit, how'd he get over here so quietly," Max said under his breath.

"Maybe he's wearing trainers," Peter said trying to stay calm.

"When you gentlemen have quite finished. Get up slowly and walk to the exit. No funny stuff, we only want to ask you a few questions," Anders said slowly.

Max got up slowly as instructed but after taking two steps spun round and threw a right jab toward the man wearing sunglasses. Max wasn't quite Mike Tyson and Anders saw the punch so early he could have sent a postcard to it, and even got a reply. As he side-stepped it connected with Peter's chin full on and sent him sprawling across a nearby table. The previously noisy café went quiet and Max stood there gasping at what he'd done. He felt a tap on his shoulder. He turned round to see a group of truck drivers who, sitting at a nearby table close by had seen the 'attack' on the young lad.

"Oi, arsehole, why don't you try someone your own size," said the first guy whose tattoos were probably the most attractive thing about him. This challenge brought a small volley of cheers from the other tables. The man stood up to face Max head on. Max glanced at Anders who had taken a step back with his hand inside his coat pocket.

'*Oh well,*' Max thought and after feigning a shrug promptly headbutted the large man in front of him square on the bridge of the nose. While he fell to his knees screaming with blood pouring from his face his mates piled in. Within the space of ten seconds the centre of the café looked like a rather violent rugby scrum. Peter slowly got his senses back and the first thing he became aware of was a damp serviette being dabbed on his face. He opened his eyes and squinted.

"My glasses," he said and began fumbling around.

"Here you go," said a soft and sweet voice. He put them on and looked at the young lady whose table he was spread over.

"Thanks," he said awkwardly. He was embarrassed and she was pretty which made it worse. She had short brown hair. She had gorgeous brown eyes and soft red lips. He realised he was staring and blushed. She smiled and blushed too. The sound of a glass being smashed on someone's head brought him abruptly back to reality.

"What's your name?" he asked quickly

"Elizabeth," she replied shyly.

"Hey, Romeo," shouted Max from near the counter. The brawl had turned into a free for all and Max was currently entwined with a bearded man in a checked shirt. Peter leapt the adjoining table and bounded across to him. He shoved his hand over the counter to try and find a weapon and found a cappuccino tube in his hand.

"Coffee?" he asked the man politely and placed the end of the tube down the collar of his shirt. He flipped the switch and the man let out a yelp and removed his hands from around Max's throat. Max jumped up and looked towards the door. There was dopey with the sunglasses again. He looked to the other side of the café at the large plate glass window and their bike, which stood on the other side of it.

"Oh bollocks," he said and ran at the window throwing his shoulder at the glass. It's amazing how far back someone bounces off a double glazed window.

"Toughened," Peter smiled as he helped Max to his feet. He grabbed one of the metal pepper pots from the counter and hit the large pane right in the bottom corner. The bang as the unit shattered was huge and Peter grinned.

"Always wanted to do that," he shouted as he jumped through the frame and clambered behind Max onto the bike. The tyres spun in the wet as they sped off. Easton stood nonchalantly against the green Jaguar as Anders ran out of the café doors.

"Very smooth," said the young man as he got into the driver's seat.

"Just stay with him," Anders growled as he slammed the door and the car squealed toward the exit.

In normal road conditions a 750cc motorcycle and a V6 Jaguar would be fairly evenly matched. However, it was raining and if you were a gambling person the word JAGUAR would be carefully etched on your betting slip. The mitigating circumstances in Max and Peter's favour were that they were two minutes ahead, there was a lot of traffic on the motorway and the bike could weave where the car could not, and British drivers have an in built fear of motorcycles and an equally strong dislike of people wealthy enough to own a Jag.

The two minutes turned into merely one on an open stretch but as they progressed to the coast, Easton could make no further gains on the bike, much to Anders' frustration. As the car squeezed through gaps most people wouldn't try and put an electric bubble car through, Anders knew better than to criticise Easton's driving. With the reverence usually reserved for fighter pilots, Easton had already gained the reputation of one of the best drivers of any four wheeled vehicle in the agency. Anders was glad to be in the passenger seat. His Baretta lay on his lap. It always had a new magazine and he had added a silencer. They were too far from the bike to get a clear shot but he wasn't unduly worried, it would only be a matter of minutes.

"Shit," exclaimed Easton as he caught the blue flashing lights of a police car in his mirror.

"Didn't you see him?" enquired a genuinely surprised Anders.

"Hell no, its an unmarked car, the blue lights are in his grill of all places," came the reply.

'What a waste of a good bullet,' Anders said to himself as he wound down his window.

A minute later two policemen stood looking at their crumpled Vauxhall sitting in a ditch by the hard shoulder wondering how on earth a car with new tyres had got such a severe puncture. Two days later a single bullet wrapped in a neat sample bag would land on an embarrassed US ambassador's desk courtesy of an extremely pissed off New Scotland Yard.

Max's mind was racing. He didn't know Southampton very well. In fact his memories of the place were very vague. He'd been on a few pub-crawls down near the dock areas whilst visiting his friend Mark at the old university down there. He smiled to himself as he remembered clambering around the shipyard after the pubs had closed. It had been winter time and the moon had given them plenty of light for exploring. They'd climbed aboard a yacht that was moored there and had been nabbed by a security guard. Ah, but the docks will have changed if Dover and Ramsgate were anything to go by. All ferries, hovercrafts, 24hr restaurants, and French speaking stewards everywhere. The commercial docks wouldn't have changed too much he hoped. He remembered lots of concrete buildings and alleys - lots of places to hide. It wasn't much of a plan but it was all he had. He caught a brief glimpse of the Jag again in his mirrors but the rain was getting heavier. They were still there. The traffic now slowly came to a standstill. His heart leapt at a sight that would normally get him mint munching. A traffic jam, which he could pass through but they couldn't. He weaved through the cars but unfortunately the jam only lasted a mile or so, it was only a shunt. He began to breathe easier, well slower at least. *'If I can only get to the next exit wherever it goes,'* he thought. It was then he saw the Jag careering up the hard shoulder.

'Bastards,' he thought *'I'll have to stay on now and go back to the original idea.'*

Easton's eyes were firmly fixed on the bike. He needed to get Anders a second or so to get a clear shot.

They passed the final exit and the motorway ended at a set of traffic lights. Red. Max was just able to see the green car about ten rows back. He edged through the first few rows until they were right on the line. It seemed like an age before the amber light came up and they shot off.

"Keep your eye on them," Easton said calmly. It was an unnecessary statement as Ander's steely eyes were fixed firmly on the bike.

"Second left," he said.

"What, the docks?" exclaimed Easton "Are they trying to catch a ship or what?"

"There is a reason," Anders said quietly as the car slid around another corner, "but I'm not sure what. Those stiffs in Washington ought to choose their decoys a little more carefully. He's still alive after run-ins with us and the IRA - not many people could lay claim to that," he added with a hint of respect.

"He can bloody ride I'll give him that," said Easton as they bounced over a mini roundabout.

Peter was in complete ignorance of the position of the car. He knew they were still with them, Max wouldn't be riding like this if they weren't. They had just passed a police car which hadn't moved. Had Max seen it? Were there more? He was itching to stick his head out and look but he knew better than that. Max had pre-warned him to stay close in and to hold on extremely tight. He had done and was still alive - which was plenty of persuasion enough. He was scared but the excitement was keeping the fear at bay.

Both Max and Anders had seen the police car. Both had noted it as unimportant to their current task in hand. By the time they reached the entrance to the commercial docks they had passed another three. Anders was still unmoved but Max was beginning to panic. *'I'd rather be locked up again then be found at the bottom of a river somewhere with a bullet in my skull,'* he thought. They squeezed past the barrier to the docks and seconds later the Jaguar shattered the barrier prompting the entrance to be quickly blocked by a number of awaiting police cars. The dock has three levels and Max took the upper one on the premise that he'd rather be forced down than up where he would have nowhere to run. Anders' window was now fully down, and the barrel of the pistol resting on the side mirror. The rain was really pouring and Max was switching from right to left. It was difficult to get a clean shot at them. The local police had the dock surrounded and as the bike and car weren't going to go anywhere they were quite content to sit tight and wait for the armed unit to arrive. Max did a neat little left and fake right and Easton lost him.

"Damn," he shouted as he slammed the gear leaver into reverse. They backtracked to the last point. Max had ridden a circle and was now riding next to the edge of the dock. To the right of them was a thirty foot drop to the bottom level and the quayside. Anders picked up the gleam of the bike off to the right and motioned Easton to stop. As the bike came into view between two buildings he grinned as he got them in his sights. He had them and squeezed the trigger.

Max felt a thud in his side and the bike toppled over the edge. As they disappeared from sight Easton sped forward and within a few seconds they had reached the point where it had gone over but as they went to get out of the car there was a large explosion. They reached the edge to see thick smoke bellowing from below. The bike had landed on a stack of fuel drums and the latter were now scattered over the quay and in the water which was alight in a number of places, as was the quayside itself. There was no sign of the bike or its riders.

"Goodbye Mr Jones," said Anders coldly as he stood in the pouring rain still sporting his sunglasses. Easton cleared his throat as he saw the dozen or so armed policemen with their guns trained on them. Anders calmly placed his gun on the bonnet, sighed and he and Easton sat on the front of the car with their hands held high. The first heavily clad figure to reach them was handed an official ID which prompted him to curse under his breath and slowly troop back to his colleagues. It would take a few minutes to check out but no doubt it would turn out to be kosher. At least they wouldn't have to clean up the mess.

The crane driver loaded the last huge crate of vodka deep into the hull of the large ship. It was near the end of his shift and even the thumping tones of Def Leppard on his headphones couldn't keep him from thinking about his tea. He picked up his copy of The Sun which had been propped open in his cab, probably the reason why he didn't notice the gaping hole in the last crate he had loaded.

***   ***   ***   ***

The two men stood motionless at attention in front of the large oak desk. No light entered the room as there were no windows and this added to the uneasy silence that had been present since they had been ushered in. The person in front of them was in a large chair behind a pile of folders and strewn documents, wearing a forced smile and had crossed arms.

"So, which one of you two marvellous gentlemen would like to explain this one away to me, eh?" The voice was stern yet feminine and its owner was a woman of forty-fiveish with straight brown hair cut into a long bob. The two men remained silent and the lady took this as a definite sign to continue.

"At the last count we had 200 policemen at the scene in Southampton, fourteen people arrested at a service station and

£15,000 pounds worth of damage there, a quay covered in bits of Honda and no definitive result."

'Oh, oh,' thought Anders, *'the search for the bodies must have been completed and come up blank.'*

"I trust you realise we are being pushed very hard to reveal the identities of the two men on the motorcycle, and before I forget Mr Anders, although the Brits haven't linked this with you I am pretty certain this is yours too," she added placing a single .35mm bullet on the desk in front of him and raising her eyebrows inquiringly. Anders stayed expressionless and spat out a regulation, "Yes Ma'am."

His unwavering response threw her a little and she continued slowly after reaching for a folder in front of her.

"I don't want to hear any talkback to this but you are both desk-bound for two weeks," she said in a determined tone. No reaction.

"If you include the car you shot off the road, we are looking at a lot of money I've got to explain away to the Brits, plus all the media speculation which we do not need. You must assume that the two 'amateurs'," she lingered on the word, "are still alive and kicking."

'Sure,' thought Easton, *'from a long drop and a fire that took three hours to put out.'*

"MI6 have confirmed that the surrounding area was combed by their people but as the body search wasn't completed until this morning they could have slipped through."

"As the sea was too rough to do the search until 36 hours afterwards, the bodies could have been washed many miles from the original spot. Besides, neither of them was exactly renowned as a powerful swimmer," said Easton.

Ms. Lamar, as she preferred to be known, looked the young man straight in the eyes and replied in a cold voice.

"I'll ignore that little outburst Mr Easton in recognition of your limited experience in the agency, and the fact that you are probably right." Still staring she added. "Nevertheless, I and my superiors have had a bellyful on this one and you boys are going to cover your asses. Besides, off the streets you are far less costly."

She handed the folder to Anders, sat back in her chair and pointed toward the door.

**** **** **** ****

'Hmm, death is cramped.' Max was semi-conscious, in complete darkness, cold and surrounded by smooth cylinders which felt like they were made of glass.

'*Ow! Yep, definitely glass.*' Exploration of his surroundings would have to be a bit more cautious. Ah, there was a soft bit. The soft bit emitted a low groan as it was prodded, and after a few more prods Max came to the conclusion that it was Peter.

"Pete," he whispered.

"Max?" came the confused reply. There was an uneasy silence as neither of them wanted to be the first to cast aspirations on their current location. Both remembered the bike crash fairly vividly but didn't know how or why they had ended up where they were. Max continued cautiously with his search and after climbing over countless bottles he reached a wall. The wall was made of wood and well able to stand up to Max banging on it. He turned around and did the same in the three other directions with the same result.

"Max," this time Peter's voice was much clearer.

"Yep," Max replied from a few feet away.

"Do you know where we are?" he asked, knowing it was a silly question.

"In a big box full of bottles, some of them broken," Max offered.

"They're vodka bottles Max - the liquid inside is a spirit, you can tell by feeling the cap, and it hasn't got much of a taste, except the burning sensation of course," Peter added.

"Very good Sherlock - you want to tell me how we got here?"

"Now that's a bit beyond me. Perhaps it's a bizarre prison cell, the product of an ill and twisted criminal mind?" Peter laughed.

"And perhaps," Max added sarcastically "God is a vodka drinker and this is his idea of purgatory."

Peter laughed again and Max joined in. As they fell silent again Peter became aware that they were moving. Well, the box that they were in was sort of moving. He didn't have much time to contemplate it as a wide shaft of light appeared above them and both covered their eyes. He could hear voices but still the light was too strong for his eyes. The voices were coming nearer and as he squinted he could see about five feet above them a hole in their box. The light came from above this opening and slowly he made out the silhouette of a couple of figures standing on top of their box peering in. Peter stood up slowly shielding his eyes from what he now guessed was the sun. As he reached his feet, his head protruded from the opening and his arms were grabbed on either side and he was hoisted up. The two men, were now distinguishable as sailors - *'We're in the hold of a ship!. Hence the movement,'* he thought. He could see through the large hold door and next to him was a ladder which led to the deck. The two sailors were in the middle of a heated discussion and kept pointing at Peter and the hole in the crate. Peter leaned over and signalled to Max to come up. Max's head popped up through the hole and he whispered to Peter.

"They're Russian, I think," he said, to which the two sailors paused and pointed at Max. As Peter struggled to help Max out of the crate one of the sailors shot up the ladder. The other produced a large knife and motioned that they should sit down, and presumably, not move. The man holding the knife looked more menacing than his weapon. He stood as tall as Max and his bare arms were as thick as tree trunks. On the left arm there were a number of tattoos including one of a knife not dissimilar to the one he was holding. The surface area of his left biceps may well have left the tattooist with a shortage of ink, as the right arm was bare, apart from the abundance of black hair that is. Max and Peter sat down without a thought and it was Max who spoke first.

"Do you remember falling off the bike?" he asked

"As I recall, you fell off and as I was attached to you I fell, too."

"Did you get the sense of falling a long way?" Max asked.

"Now that you mention it, as we parted company with the bike the ground just seemed to open up."

"Yeah, we were over the edge of the quay. I can only assume that somehow we landed on this crate."

"I won't even begin to try and work that one out," Peter said shaking his head slowly.

"But how did we come to fall off the bike?" he added.

"That's the weird thing," Max replied. "It felt like a push, almost as if I had been shot, but I can't feel any pain."

Peter looked worried. "It could have hit a nerve and you could be bleeding or getting infected, or anything." At this he stood slowly and checked Max over. He could feel the tattoo man's eyes following his every move but he carried on.

"Hey, that's my wallet," Max chuckled as Peter felt his right hip pocket. As he worked his way round to the left one he saw a neat round hole and paused. There was a large damp patch around the hole.

"OK, I've found it," he said in a serious voice. Max stopped smiling as Peter reached behind the jeans. Max clenched his teeth and as he squinted his eyes he actually looked quite constipated. He opened his eyes as he heard Peter start laughing loudly. He was holding Max's now very dented hip flask. He held it up to Max's face and Max saw the bullet firmly embedded in the antique silver. He took the flask and after putting it under great scrutiny shook it and declared,

"Good job, it's still got some left in it," to which Peter frowned.

"Well, it's 18 year old malt, bloody good stuff," he added.

Their relief was cut short by a short burst of Russian and the threatening waving of the knife. Their friend with the tattoo didn't know what these mad Englishmen were up to but he suspected it had something to do with being locked up in a box for two days. They seemed to calm down after his actions which was just as well as the most savage act committed with the knife to date was the butchery of a batch of innocent cabbages and cauliflowers. He was the cook but these two dimwits were thankfully unaware of this. He was as puzzled as his crewmate on how the hell they ended up in the hold. Still, it was the captain's problem and no doubt he would show his face soon enough.

Max and Peter sat quietly with fairly cheerful expressions on their faces. Max fiddled with his penknife trying to free the bullet from the flask. It was a fairly large one as hip flasks go - leather and silver and engraved 'Good Luck Max - Croydon Branch' except now it was C.........n Branch. He'd been given it fifteen years ago when he had left a company south of the river. Peter watched intently and was as engrossed with the retrieval as Max. Neither of them noticed the well-built, well-dressed man come down the ladder and stand before them.

Captain Yarun was his name and he was one of the two crew members on the ship that spoke a bit of English.

"Good afternoon, gentlemen," he said in an impeccable southern counties' accent.

Max and Peter were startled at the sound of their own language and immediately embarrassed at not noticing the arrival of their host. They both stood up and Max extended his hand which was shaken firmly. It quickly became apparent that the greeting delivered so expertly constituted most of the captain's vocabulary. They managed to glean that he wanted to know what they were doing on his ship. They were as much in the dark on that subject as he was and after lots of explaining, including animated visual displays, the captain reluctantly accepted that he was stuck with these two for the remainder of the voyage. He hauled the other English speaker - a small kitchen hand called Balof whose mastery of the English language strayed into double figures word-wise. It was from him that Peter enquired their port of destination. They eventually received the reply of 'Newcastle' but from his rantings they assumed it was a round-about route. This was fine with them as the captain had sent for a mop and bucket and knife and fork and had demonstrated in a bizarre form of charades that they could earn their keep on the ship. The deal was struck over a bottle of vodka taken from the very crate they had begun the journey in.

Easton sat patiently behind a desk full of papers in a small hotel room in Southampton which they had hastily converted into a temporary office. A laptop computer with a small printer attached sat on the desk in front of him and it was this that held his attention. Anders sat in one of the armchairs reading 'The Times' - he didn't care too much for computers but had to admit that they made things easier. Easton was a whiz on those things and as he read, he could hear Easton tapping away furiously once more. They had been there for two days now compiling all the possible routes out of Southampton. There was still no sign of the bodies but that didn't worry him. They would stay here for another few more days, file a report then head home. Job done. The tapping stopped and Easton stood up and went to the kitchen. He emerged a couple of moments later with two steaming cups of coffee. Anders set the paper down and carefully spooned three spoons of brown sugar into the mug and looked over at Easton who was now setting the printer in motion. The Brits had done themselves proud keeping all this out of the papers. None had linked the bike chase with Max Jones though some had mentioned it briefly. The Times had run a piece on how sources of theirs had suggested the fugitive had fled abroad. Anders was pleased with this as it would remove any further attention in the UK.

"That's the ship report," Easton said as he sat down. He flicked through the sheets of printer paper as he sipped his coffee.

"A grand total of two hundred and twelve vessels, of twenty seven nationalities."

"How many destinations?" Anders enquired casually.

"Seventeen," replied Easton.

"Ouch," came the reaction to that.

"That's quite a few countries to cover. Lots of paperwork," he added shaking his head.

"Yep, I suppose we'd better get onto it. There are seven major nations and ten minor. What do you fancy?"

"I'll take the majors," Anders replied in an apathetic tone. It made sense though. Anders had more contacts in the big countries than Easton and they covered over a hundred and fifty of the ships on the list. It was a boring routine. They would contact the local agencies in those countries, quote the ships to check and sit back and wait. They had missed four ships that had already reached their destinations but the next one didn't arrive until tomorrow. He'd been in England for three months now, and despite the long phone calls to Cassie his fiancee, Easton was getting fed up. She was marvellous, a trainee lawyer with gorgeous blonde locks that cascaded over her shoulders. They planned to get hitched at the end of the year. It seemed so close. She had accepted his career quite easily as she worked long hours and studied endlessly so didn't have too much free time either. He looked over at Anders engrossed in his paper. *'Not the ideal stand-in partner,'* he thought. *'About as much conversation as a trappist monk on valium.'* This last thought made him smile as he tapped a few more keys and brought up the fax module. Two hours later the contacts had been made and the wheels set slowly in motion.

**** **** **** ****

"Fishk!" was the greeting as the cook's mate placed two steaming plates in front of Max and Peter. The latter dived straight in pausing only to salt his potatoes. Max sat and looked at the stew sitting on the long table in the dining area. He hated fish - he always had, and it was all they had eaten in the last four days. He was also concerned that their journey was taking so long. Every time he ventured onto deck (which wasn't very often) either the visibility was atrocious or all he could see was blue sea and sky. Peter was loving every minute. He'd grown up on fish apparently and had found that the main activity on the ship was chess, which naturally the little sod was bloody good at. He had to admit though that their hosts had been very good and he couldn't swear that had he been in captain Yarun's position he wouldn't have just chucked them overboard. He made up his mind to try and find out more about their route. They had docked once but decided that it was better to wait until Newcastle to jump ship. In return for their passage they were basically doing any task that needed doing. He had spent yesterday afternoon peeling spuds and this morning in the boiler room helping out the engineers. Last night had proved to be a scream. Some crew members had decided on a bit of a party and the living area which normally consisted of rows of bunks dimly lit and dingy had been transformed into racks of bunks less dimly lit, a cassette player and a crate of vodka. The music consisted solely of 'The Beetlies' as they affectionately referred to them. Within an hour they were all singing along with the words. He was sure he would never forget the rendition of 'She loves you yeah yeah yeah'. That vodka was good stuff too as his head kept reminding him. Oh yes, and after the singing came the dancing, well sort of. Max had insisted, he couldn't remember why, on learning Cossack dancing. The lads readily agreed to teach him and a slightly reluctant Peter also took part. Abbot and Costello, Laurel and Hardy and even the Marx Brothers could all have learnt from them last night. When he wasn't knocking tables over it was people he was toppling. He landed on his bum more times than he would care to mention. He couldn't remember getting back to his bunk but Peter had told him that three of the crew members had carried him there. He ate the last forkful of lunch and had to concede that as fish went that was pretty good. Peter had long finished and was already into a game of chess with one of the officers. They had the afternoon and the evening to themselves and Max decided he would pop up and see the captain. This was a bit of a drawn out routine as he had to communicate his wish to one of the crew who then arranged for him to go above deck. The first few times had been tougher as the word 'captain' meant nothing to most of them and Max had to resort to mime again. Now he asked one of them who disappeared and returned within a couple of minutes nodding his head. The captain's cabin was at the head of the ship almost directly behind the bridge. He was seated at his desk looking at some charts when Max entered. He rose and beamed shaking Max's hand firmly.

"Sit, sit," he said and pointed toward an armchair. As Max went to sit down he saw the laid out charts and stopped. The one on top showed the African continent and the surrounding seas. Curious, Max pointed at the map and shrugged his shoulders. The captain pointed at the cape and said simply.

"Last night, dock."

You could have knocked Max over with a feather. He tried to hide his shock, swallowed hard and asked enquiringly,

"Newcastle?"

Captain Yarun smiled and reached for another chart. This one showed South East Asia and Australia.

"Newcastle," said the captain pointing at a large town north of Sydney on Australia's east coast. He pointed to a dotted red line, which led from there under Tasmania and out into the ocean.

The ship's doctor could find nothing wrong with the Englishman and no reason as to why he should be so white. He had fainted for no apparent reason whilst talking to the captain.

'These bloody English can't hold their vodka,' he thought as he handed the big man a cup of coffee.

**** **** **** ****

"Keep tabs on them. I want to know everything they do. Be careful though, they may appear like two monumental screw-ups but they are actually two of the agency's best." *'And lord help the agency if that's true,'* he thought as he turned back to his scrawled notes on the blackboard.

"Anders," he continued, "is a bit of a slippery bastard but basically clean. Easton could do TV commercials for detergent and be the cleanest thing on the screen." He paused looking at the small group in front of him. They were young, by his standards and still eager. He felt annoyed at giving them another 'no result' assignment but they had to be kept busy - his superiors had already begun hinting that 'staff cuts' were on the way. He continued, "If something stinks," the *if* echoed in the minds of each of them, "my instinct tells me it will be further up. As usual this is a closed unit. The room is clear and the brief is unknown outside these four walls." At this last remark he nodded toward his superior who occupied a seat behind the group. At first, his penchant for sitting in on the briefings had irritated Martin, but he'd got used to it.

"Don't dig too hard until you get something, but when you do I'll be waiting. The detail, and there is a stack of it, is in the folders. They also include everything I have told you this morning in case any of you had a rough one last night." He glanced at Perez as he said the last remark which broke a few smiles. Perez was teetotal and she'd had many a comment like that thrown her way. Drinking was an accepted part of the life of an internal affairs agent. At least it had been in the predominantly male dominated agency. Martin was one of the 'Old School' who took the influx of a number of excellent female recruits into the teams with difficulty. The fact that she didn't share their love of beer, whiskey or indeed baseball made her a prime target for smartass remarks. They seldom went further than that though as the ladies had proved that they were more than holding their own. Angie Perez was no exception, and had plenty of respect from her four male colleagues. The team had been together nine months and worked very well. The department now covered all law enforcement and other agencies. The most identifiable success to date had been cracking a powerful corruption ring in the Chicago police force six months ago. The last dozen or so assignments had come up empty. This was positive of course in that those being investigated came up clean, but made the team feel that their efforts were misdirected. They were given a week at the beginning of each case for initial investigation, and at the end of if nothing had surfaced then they moved onto the next one. Not an ideal method but these were the days of 'efficiency' and 'correct use of the taxpayers dollar.' The meeting closed, and as with all the cases before it, the team left to individually examine the facts.

Four hours later they met up again. This time the venue was the back of a poolroom downtown. Sam Matthews, the most senior of the team stood up and the others hushed. At six foot four he was also the tallest member with light brown hair and blue eyes. It was his ability and leadership that held the respect of the group not his size. He spoke as he always did, clearly and with authority.

"Well, two of the team will stay here in The States. Unless there are any other suggestions, Andrew and Juan would be my choice." There were nods of agreement. "Angie, Tom and myself will head to England and keep tabs on these two guys from there."

"You think there's anything in it?" The question came from Tom Jilney, a tall athletic man with blond hair whose gold rimmed spectacles looked peculiar set against his large frame.

"Its difficult to say," replied Sam.

"There are a number of things which puzzle me," he added to murmurs of agreement. "But I'd like to hear what you all think first."

The first to speak up was Juan Manilt. He was Puerto-Rican by descent and a virtual wizard with anything electronic. He had classic dark Latin looks and a deep lightly accented voice in which he continued.

"The official word from the agency is that the two are in England to add weight to the search for Max Jones after initially going there as chaperones for some research work."

"Correct," replied Sam.

"Yet, from the accounts of the events at Southampton it appeared that they planned to take Jones back in a wooden box."

"That's a bit presumptuous," argued Tom.

"Anders and Easton would argue that dealing with someone like Jones you had to be ready to strike first," he suggested.

"Except that he had a hostage," added Juan.

"That hasn't always stopped the agency before," said Angie with a solemn face.

Juan nodded and said, "Our sources add that they are putting considerable effort in the possibility that Jones is still alive and kicking."

"So they screwed up and now they've got some desk duty for being bad boys?" Sam said casually standing up and pacing around.

"I think it's one of two things. Either, as you say, the agency has assumed Jones is dead and the continued activity is to make a point," he paused, "or there is another reason they want him and they can't ignore the possibility that he is still alive."

"No chance." It was the first time that Andrew Kettles had spoken. He was a fairly quiet man with mousy hair, small frame and a razor sharp mind.

"They think he's dead. The reason I'm so sure is that that they are searching, but not very hard."

Angie smiled and nodded, "Yeah, they've not put the net completely tight out there," she agreed. Sam nodded and took control of the meeting again.

"OK. So we have two agents who outpace the rest of the forces to find this guy. Then they screw up and lose him once in Berkshire. Then they find him again only this time they are a little too eager to stop him getting away and making themselves look stupid again." He put the facts out as the agency would have done themselves.

"I don't buy it," Angie said. "They've been sent on a mission which should have been classed level two, for some reason given a high level three and they are putting far too much into it. I know the situation with Northern Ireland is a biggie, what with the large Irish contingent over here, but there must be another reason why they want him."

Sam grinned. That was the second time Angie had snapped at him more energetically than normal. *'This'll be a long opening meeting,'* he thought and made a note to try and find out what else was on her mind.

****　　****　　****　　****

The sun was setting and demanding everyone's attention. The clear sky, calm water and still wind assured it would get it.

Max stood on the upper deck smiling at the beautiful shimmering bay that stretched before him. Barely a mile away the hustle and bustle of the busy port seemed like the other side of the world. He fidgeted uncomfortably in the unfamiliar outfit that sat snugly on his large frame. Dark blue trousers, black boots and a thick navy sweater, Max the Russian sailor. The outfit was topped off with a navy bobble hat. He hadn't shaved for a week and a half and had a rough look about him. He was happy with the way he looked, it was the language that he was worried about. In order to get past immigration at the docks the captain had arranged for him and Peter to assume the identities of two of the crew. To this end Peter's hair had been shaven to make him look similar to one of the kitchen hands. Large sailors with beards and dark hair seem to be in abundance in Russia so Max had no problem finding someone he resembled. All of the ship's crew had 'day passes' which enabled them to leave the ship whilst it was in dock unloading. The two members whose identities they were using would be concealed and thus the full quota of crew would pass through immigration in one bunch including Max and Peter. Neither of the two selected spoke any English, which was probably an advantage. He hoped and prayed that none of the customs men spoke Russian. To get them by they had spent the last two days learning as much as they could. The method was simple. They went for accuracy rather than vocabulary or grammar. They found those words which they could pronounce perfectly and ignored those which they had been hopeless at. The result was a mix-match of words and phrases that sounded foreign but would have any Russian speaker questioning their sanity. They had got the names down to a tee and also a few English words with a heavy Russian accent. Yet again Peter had taken to it like a duck to water and was reeling off whole sentences like a pro. It felt warm for evening. *'The channel isn't much like this,'* he thought as he turned and looked out to sea. There was very little cloud and in the distance he could make out the horizon. It was as if an artist had painted the two lines in blue in front of him, only the bottom one had been done with an old brush and had left yellow streaks. He smiled to himself as he thought of his wife and their honeymoon. Clacton 1972. They, too, had a sunset like this though the wind never really dies down over there. They had huddled together on the beach with a steaming flask of milky tea, sitting there eating fish & chips. For a moment he stopped smiling as he thought of her home alone in London. His mind returned to his next move. Max the sailor would soon have to turn into Max the 'interested neurologist' writing a PhD. He was sure Australia had someone somewhere that could help him. *'Probably on the other bloody side,'* he thought as he returned to 'below deck' ready to dock.

**** **** **** ****

The meeting lasted a little over three hours and as Sam said goodbye to his colleagues he put a hand gently on Angie's shoulder.

"Have you got a minute?" he asked politely. Things had become increasingly awkward between them and he felt it was only a matter of time before the team was going to be affected.

"Sure, but I'd rather not talk here," Angie replied. Sam shrugged and as they walked down the stairs to the main bar he suggested a coffee back at his apartment which was only a couple of blocks down from hers. Angie nodded and smiled for the first time that evening and they headed out into the night air.

After an uneventful but very wet journey across town, Sam unlocked the door to his top floor apartment. It was in a small block in what could be best described as a cosmopolitan area. Despite being 3am the sound of the city still wide awake on the street below drifted up into the open plan living area. On the left as they came in was the kitchen where Sam headed, coming to a stop in front of the fridge. He turned around after checking inside.

"Er, is black coffee all right?" he asked.

"Sure," Angie smiled. The room was big and with the large windows she imagined it would be bright in the daytime. The couch was simple and modern, as was most of the furniture. Organised, clean and tidy but definitely lacking a woman's touch. She had never been to Sam's apartment before but had often imagined what it would be like. The only item standing out was a sideboard along the back wall past the iron circular staircase that led to the second level. It was about six feet long, dark, old, and looked extremely heavy. "It was my father's," Sam said handing over the steaming mug of coffee into her hands. "It's been in my family for years. My father died ten years ago and as the only child I've sort of inherited it."

"Where did it come from originally?" asked Angie. She wasn't really interested but wanted to know anything about the man in front of her.

"England. It was made in the 1800s and my great grandfather bought it in the 1890s as a wedding present to my great grandmother."

Angie smiled and sat down beside him on the couch. There was an awkward silence with both of them clutching their coffee mugs and staring down at the dark contents. "We need to talk," Angie said quietly into her coffee.

'She's so beautiful. Even with her hair soaked,' Sam thought as he looked at her. He put a finger to her lips and

kissed her gently on the forehead. Angie sighed as if a huge weight had been lifted from her shoulders.

"How did you know," she asked.

"I wasn't sure," Sam replied, "but you never look me in the eyes these days," he laughed softly. He placed an arm around her and she rested her head on his shoulder.

"You do know there's no way anything can come of this," Sam said quietly.

"Yes," replied Angie as she turned around and kissed him.

**** **** **** ****

They didn't have to wait too long moored out on the bay. Captain Yarun had a call on the radio that he could now dock. It was 7pm. They had been expected the following day but calm seas had meant that they were ahead of time. As they neared the dock Max and Peter said goodbye to their newly found comrades. Peter had arranged with two of them to play chess by correspondence which had amused and pleased the captain. In a mere five minutes they would be off the ship and in the hands of customs. The photographs on the passports were old and faded and they were quite confident. The language side still niggled Max. *'Can we pull it off?'* he thought. He felt the side of the ship knock the dock and finally come to a stop. The gangway was being lowered and the crew climbed the ladder to the deck, the two impostors with them, out into the evening light. They crossed the deck in a quiet procession and the rusty sheet gangplank rattled as they trooped across it. As the thirty or so men crossed the quay to the inviting glow of the customs offices Max looked back at the ship. It was the first and last time he would see the vessel that had carried them half the way around the world. It was an imposing black colour and in the faint light he could just distinguish the areas covered in rust, basically most of the hull. *'I'm glad I saw it like this,'* he mused. *'Probably looks like just another rust bucket by day,'* he thought. They reached the doors of the Australian Customs Authority. Once inside they treaded the dull grey carpet toward the long queues by the security gates. They funnelled quickly through with their possessions, passing through the regulation x-ray machines. Max beeped profoundly as he walked through the gate finding it was his hip flask, pen knife and bullet (which had been tastefully crafted into a key-ring whilst on board). He smiled and shrugged at the security guard who simply sighed and held out the little dish while he passed through again. *'Dopey sailors,'* Max guessed he was thinking, and he wasn't far off. The easy part was over with and they rounded the corner and a bright yellow sign gleamed out at them - Immigration. Max followed the rest of the crew who had all joined the queue on the far left. He glanced at each of the officials in turn. They all looked bored out of their skulls. Most of the sailors passing through appeared to be foreign and there was very little dialogue. The bunch in the queue next to them was Italian and the one next to that Spanish. Further across the room were a few queues full of young Asian sailors. All denominations, colours and creeds standing in lines; quiet as mice they were being ushered through at the rate of two a minute. As he came nearer to the front of the queue he noticed there were two officers and the people in the line went to each in turn. They had another group ahead of them, which was just going through now. The first of their crew went to the left hand officer and went straight through. Now the other side - Max couldn't quite see but this one took a little longer, or was it his imagination. As he got closer he could hear why. The sod on the right could speak a little Russian and no doubt out of sheer boredom was having great fun practising. The odds against both he and Peter getting the guy on the left were pretty high. There was nothing they could do. He looked at the clock. 7:20pm. Peter would notice in a minute or two. How would he feel?

Peter had already noticed and was suppressing his panic. Suddenly all he had learnt in the last few days had gone all fuzzy. He breathed deeply and focused on the collar of the man in front of him. He was a tall man and Peter's eyes were at the same level as the collar. It was a pretty clean collar *'But he's got pretty bad dandruff,'* he thought. He tried to close his mind to his surroundings. It wasn't working.

Max was now three from the front. It could go either way. One to the left, one to the right. *'Come on, come on,'* Max urged the guy on the left to hurry up. He was aware that he was sweating and a bead had settled on his left eyebrow. "Next." It was the man on the left. *'Thank God,'* Max thought and stepped up to the counter handing over his passport and papers. The customs officer was slightly balding and had thick round glasses which had slid halfway down his nose.

"Good Evening," he said without looking up

"Cabbage and Gravy, Saucepan," said Max quietly in perfect Russian. The man looked up and smiled handing the papers back to Max.

"Next," he called as Max walked down the corridor. One down, one to go.

Peter was still focused on the man in front's collar. He was close to the front. He calculated that if they went through one by one like this he would get the one on the right. He was willing the pattern to change but left, right, left right it went and it wasn't going to change. He was close now, only one person. The dandruff man between him and doom. "Next." It was the man on the left. He was now at the front of the queue. It would be soon. Any second now. He stared into space in front of him. "Next," came the call. Hold on a minute, it was the man on the left. He was still frozen to the spot. "Next," called the man again and Peter walked quickly to the counter fumbling with the papers.

"Good Evening," came the greeting from the top of the man's head.

"I'd like my steak well done," replied Peter - perfect accent.

'It's the first one that came into my head,' he thought. The man smiled and nodded and gave back the papers. As Peter turned he could hear the man with the other officer having a heated argument which must have gone on for a few minutes. The sailor growled and followed after Peter and as he did so winked at him. The other officer shouted something after them and Peter wondered what it was. The translation later in a small café was along the lines of "And you can tell those smart asses with the food orders that some of us do speak Russian....."

**** **** **** ****

The sunlight woke Sam and he yawned. He blinked the tiredness away from his eyes to see Angie's slender figure slipping into a white blouse and a pair of jeans. She was standing in the bathroom and paused to look in the mirror unaware he was awake.

"Sleep OK?" Sam asked.

"Fine," she replied but he knew she was lying.

"Do you want to go for breakfast somewhere?" he asked trying to break her mood.

"No thanks. I'll, er, see you later," she said as she headed out of the door.

"Angie," he called after her but heard her shoes clanging on the staircase and the apartment door close behind her. Sam lay back in the bed and stared at the ceiling. *'What is it with me and women?'* he thought. *'I'm crazy about a beautiful woman who for once cares for me too, and she ends up sleeping on my couch and treating me like a stranger.'*

**** **** **** ****

With three days worth of stubble, Easton looked somewhere between a sleep-deprived stock-broker and a Manhattan tramp. They'd had nothing positive back from any of their contacts. False alarms were into double figures and were frustrating as none looked even vaguely like the pictures of Jones that they had faxed out. Anders had been irritable since the previous Tuesday, stomping around like a caged animal. They were wasting their time. They knew it, their bosses knew it and perhaps many of their transatlantic colleagues knew it too. He missed the smell of Cassie's perfume, especially on her robe. All he could smell at the moment was Anders' after shave which was definitely tinged with a canine element. It was a poky little room too. Lounge, kitchen and dining room all rolled into one. The seats were comfortable though. Oh yes, and the TV only had four channels. He didn't watch much back home but he knew there was always a minimum of fifty. There had been a good 'Duke' movie on a couple of days back. Anders idolised John Wayne and wouldn't hear a word against him. Easton quite liked the slow drawling voice too. Still, all of this would be over by the morning. Just a few more ships had docked that day and the fax remained silent. *'It will take a while to shake this one off,'* he thought and remembered back to Colonel Masters' words, "cushy assignment" and repeated them over in his head. It would be an embarrassing return to the US. He was young though and there would be many more missions. He looked out of the window at a rain soaked scene. "I hope the next one is somewhere a damn sight sunnier," he murmured to himself.

**** **** **** ****

Across the street in a similar hotel room three people sat playing cards. They had been there two days. They were bored too. Tom rose from the table and grabbed the coffee jug from the counter. He poured another mugful for Sam and himself but Angie placed her hand over her mug saying, "That'd be my tenth and I hate to go into double figures in any one day."

Tom chuckled and added, "I wonder if our two laughing chums would like some?"

"Probably," said Sam "from what we know, they are coming up empty on their traces and they have been cooped up for ages."

"Poor bastards," said Tom, "everyone screws up once in a while."

"Well, they are certainly having plenty of time to contemplate their fates," nodded Angie solemnly. She avoided Sam's eyes again and tried to focus on her cards.

"Yep, I wouldn't fancy being in their shoes when they get back to face the big cheeses," said Sam sipping at his coffee.

"Jesus this stuff's strong Tom," he winced.

"Yeah, just how I like it - oh, full house by the way," he said laying down his hand in a neat fan shape. The other two threw in their cards and shook their heads. Tom was on a roll again.

***   ***   ***   ***

The hostel they had stayed in had eaten up $40 of the $600 they had managed to get from Peter's visa card. It was risky to leave any trace, but without money they could do nothing. Besides, they would be well out of Newcastle by this time tomorrow. They were standing outside the central library. The only brief stop they had made was to a charity shop in town. They were both kitted out in jeans and T shirts. The library was a modern building with lots of red brick and glass. They walked through the automatic doors and were greeted with a friendly smile from the lady at reception. After a brief bout of questions she pointed them towards the periodical section.

"What were you on about CDs for?" Peter said puzzled as they climbed the stairs.

Max tried not to appear patronising.

"Well, some of the magazines and journals have made it onto CD ROM and progressive libraries often carry a good selection," He paused as he reached the top of the stairs.

"You mean your newspaper doesn't use CD ROMs at all?" he asked.

"Nope. We've got a word processor but only Milly really knows how to use that," Peter smiled.

'At last,' Max thought, *'something he isn't an expert on'.*

As they reached the periodicals section they saw a small bespectacled man in a collar, tie and cardigan tidying the already quite ordered desk in front of him. He was almost devoid of hair and the top of his head gleamed as he put the items into their places meticulously.

"Good morning," said Max cheerfully.

"How can I help you?" replied the man casting a critical eye over the two of them. How he wished they could introduce a dress code.

"We are looking for any medical journals that you have on CD, please."

The little man did very little to conceal his obvious surprise.

"Are you quite sure?" he asked with a good deal of sarcasm.

"Yep," said Peter quickly before Max could retaliate.

"Ok," the man said slowly, "Have you operated one of these before," he sneered confident that these two would be blissfully ignorant.

"Well," answered Max, "it appears to be a standard Panasonic 2400 quad speed windows driven drive and I believe you are running a HP multi-level menu system allowing random access and multi-search print with storage of multiple data blocks." Max smiled, managing not to sound smug which seemed to annoy the little man even more. He stared at them for a moment then reached into a locked drawer and promptly brought out three CD ROM cases.

"AMA Journal, Modern Medicine and Medicine Today," he said flatly.

Max smiled, picked them up, and again before he could speak Peter piped up.

"Thank you very much," he said quickly and ushered Max toward the waiting machine.

"I didn't know you knew about computers," Peter said quietly as they sat down in front of the PC.

"Just don't tell anyone," Max grinned, "it'd ruin my reputation."

The PC stirred into life and Max loaded the first CD. The menus flicked by as Max tapped away at the keyboard. Peter watched engrossed as Max searched under lots of criteria. 'Neurology', 'Brain Tissue' and so on. It was the term 'cerebral' that came up with the greatest number of articles. He scanned the titles quickly as he went through them on the screen he marked those for printing that he thought might be useful. Then came the next CD and finally the third. After each one he set the printer in motion and by the end the inkjet printer on the next desk had a neat pile of printouts in the tray. Max piled up the CDs and returned them to the counter where the little man was still in an irritable mood. When he returned, he gave Peter half the pile and they moved to a quiet corner.

"OK," said Max in a whisper, "I'm looking for any notable brain experts who appear in the articles - mark them and where they practice or lecture."

Peter nodded and picked up the first article. He was really beginning to admire this big man. Many in his position would have given up a long time ago but he had this dogged determination and ability to think rationally in the oddest situations. They both sat in silence for what seemed like an hour, but was closer to two. Max finished ahead of Peter and helped with his pile. They had come up with a list of eleven and Max noted them on a plain piece of paper.

"To the phones," Max said emphatically and bounded down the stairs two at a time, which drew a glare from the little bald man. He stopped at reception for directions and a $10 phone card. The phone booths were around the corner and Max turned to Peter as they left the building.

"Look, if I get to work on these maybe you can grab us some lunch." He motioned to the shopping mall at the end of the street.

"Okay," said Peter happily. He was glad to get out in the fresh air again. Max found the phones and set about finding the experts. Directories gave him the numbers and he started phoning around the hospitals and two universities. By the time he reached number nine on the list he was beginning to despair a little. Six were now in the states, two had died and one's whereabouts they did not know. He keyed in number ten.

"Hello, South Adelaide State Hospital can I help you?"

"I'm looking for Dr Bradshaw."

"Which department please?" came the terse reply.

"Neurology?" he replied hesitantly.

The phone clicked and started ringing again. It seemed to go on for ages.

"Neurology," said the gruff voice. It sounded like the other person was out of breath.

"Yes, hello, I'm looking for Dr Bradshaw. I believe he works in your department."

"Bradshaw. Bradshaw, doesn't ring a bell," said the young voice.

"Hey Joe, do you know a Dr Bradshaw?" he shouted across the room. Max waited patiently as a brief discussion ensued.

"He used to be the boss here apparently, but he's been retired 2 years now."

Max sighed *'I guess asking won't hurt,'* he thought.

"Any idea what happened to him?"

"Hold on," said the young man who had now regained his breath. Max waited for the negative reply.

"Hi there. My name's Joe. I used to work with the good doctor - can I ask who you are?" The voice was much older and Max had to think quickly.

"James Hughes. I'm doing my doctorate on a new neurological theory. I read some of his work and would have loved to speak to him."

"Hey, you're a pomme, right?"

"Yes I am," Max said in his best Queen's English.

"I'm only here for two weeks doing some research. You wouldn't happen to know where he lives now?" he asked hopefully.

"Sure. I reckon the doc would be flattered. Hold on a moment, I've got it written down somewhere." Max waited eagerly, pen poised.

"Here you go, Napperby.....," Max took down the full details and repeated them slowly.

"Du Rhone Homestead, Empty Creek Road, Napperby near Alice Springs. Ok, how near is near?" he asked tentatively.

"About 150kms Northwest I think," came the reply.

"How about a phone?" Max asked hopefully.

"Phone?" the other man laughed.

"He hasn't got a phone. He wanted to get away from civilisation after his wife died. Why do you think he's living in the middle of nowhere? We get a letter from him now and again. Seems pretty happy out there. If you see him, tell him Joe says Hi."

"I'd be glad to," Max said making a few more notes, "and thanks."

"No worries mate," replied the old male nurse as he put the phone down. *'Hmm'* Max thought. *'This sounds like quite a distance'.* He decided to try the last one on the list. Two minutes afterward the name had a line through it with 'Deceased' scribbled next to it.

"Well Dr Bradshaw," Max said to himself, "I guess you'll just have to do." He carefully folded the page of notes and as he put it into his pocket he saw Peter crossing the street grinning. In one hand held aloft was a brown paper bag and in the other about a dozen packets of extra strong mints.

****   ****   ****   ****

'For once,' Easton thought, *'he really does need those sunglasses.'* He looked across at Anders and then out of the window again. The airport bus from La Guardia reaches the corner of 46th and 8th in twenty minutes on a good day. It wasn't a good day, and they had been on the bus close to an hour. To add to the frustration, the air conditioning didn't work and the occupants of the bus smelt like a wrestler's armpit -

after a bout. It was with great relief they clambered off the bus into the 35° heat and made their way down 8th Street dressed once more in their dull grey suits. As they approached the nondescript cream coloured building, Easton did his top button up and straightened his tie. Anders, the perpetual martyr, had gone the whole bus journey without touching his collar. They passed the polished brass plate that read 'Southern Electrical Units' and crossed to the reception. *'Now for the usual games,'* Easton thought.

"Good Afternoon gentlemen," said the stout dark-haired man from behind the counter.

Easton smiled and said, "We have a meeting with Mr Lexington-Smythe at 2pm." The man looked at his watch. It was 3pm.

"You're early then," he said quizzically.

"Yes a little." replied Easton, "Do you have anywhere we can freshen up?" he said trying to sound serious. The man smiled and handed him a piece of paper. Easton thanked him and they sat down on a bench next to a row of phones. He opened the note - *'Right hand lift - second floor. Press emergency button and wait twenty seconds.'* Easton read it slowly, took a lighter from his breast pocket and lit the corner. He waited till the flames almost touched his fingers and placed it in the ashtray. They both rose and walked to the lifts. The second lift opened invitingly and they stepped in. Anders looked at Easton and pressed the 2 button firmly. Easton shrugged and when they reached the second floor he waited until the doors closed again and pressed the emergency button. The lights cut out and they were in darkness. The lift lurched downward and they couldn't tell how far down they had gone when it came to a stop. They waited. Soon a small light came on and a panel on the left-hand side opened revealing what looked like an entrance to a vent shaft. Easton sighed and put his bag through the hole and followed it on his hands and knees. Anders did the same. After twenty feet or so of crawling they came to a tunnel twice the size of the one they had been in. Immediately in front of them was what seemed like a go-cart only it had no wheels. It had two seats and a panel with two traced hand shapes on it.

'This gets worse,' Easton thought as he put the bag into the cart and placed his right hand on the screen. As Anders placed his hand on too, there was a succession of flickering lights and a couple of beeps. As they felt some minor vibrations Anders spoke.

"Mind your ....(smack) head." Too late. The dull thud of Easton's head against the sloping ceiling echoed around them.

"Shit!" came the quick reply. Easton looked over at Anders bent forward in his seat. The cart was hovering in mid-air.

"Magnetic field," said Anders smugly as the cart shot forward. The ride lasted a mere two minutes in which time the tunnel had veered left and right so many times they couldn't begin to guess where they had ended up. It was a small room with a single door.

'And a proper frigging ceiling,' Easton thought. They stood up and straightened their suits. The door opened onto a well-lit corridor and a succession of well armed MPs stood at attention beside each door.

"Colonel Masters is expecting you, sirs," said one of them with a firm salute.

'Yippee,' thought Easton and walked to the steel door which the MP had opened slightly. Colonel Masters had his back to them as they entered the room. They stood to attention and the Colonel waited for the click of the door closing before he turned around. He wasn't smiling.

'Ok, do your worst,' Easton thought uneasily.

"It gives me great sadness gentlemen to have to give you these," he said handing them each a sealed white envelope. Both held the envelopes for a moment and then opened them. The Colonel continued.

"Sadness, because if I had my way I'd slap you two dimwits so hard I'd have to redecorate afterwards," he said calmly. Easton reached inside the envelope to find an airline ticket. He glanced at Anders and opened up the ticket. Sydney? He felt and looked a little puzzled. The Colonel spoke again.

"While the two of you were on the bus from the airport I got a call. Our friend Mr Jones and his sidekick are alive and well in Australia. It means you have one more chance and I have to shelve the dressing down I was going to give you." He said with a wry smile. Easton didn't know what to say, neither, come to that did, Anders.

'At least it'll be hot there,' Easton thought.

**** **** **** ****

The brown bag had contained a number of hot pasties of varying descriptions. Max went for a contrast, a traditional 'Cornish' and a 'Mexican'. The latter turned out to be a disappointing mix of hamburger mince and kidney beans. They were sitting in the food hall of a large shopping mall. In front of Peter was a steaming coffee as yet untouched. Max's cup was all but empty and Peter got up to get another. Max reached into his pocket and lifted out the map they had bought at the newsagent on the way in. He carefully folded it out and found that no matter which way he turned it a good part was draped over the edge of the table. Peter returned with the second cup of coffee and grinned as he saw Max poring over the map.

"You haven't told me where we're off to next," he said as he sat down.

"Alice Springs," Max answered with very little enthusiasm.

"Good one," Peter chuckled. "But seriously, where are we off to?"

"Napperby, near Alice Springs," Max said irritably. He was having trouble finding the place on the map. Peter realised he was serious and slowly placed a finger on Alice Springs in the centre of the map. Max was still looking at the bottom right hand corner and it took him a few moments for him to notice Peter's hand. He glanced over, paused and checked the scale of the map. A quiet ten seconds passed as his eyes made out the distance between them and their new destination.

"One thousand, four hundred miles," he said slowly.

"Crocodile Dundee may have hidden from the mob in the bush, but at least he was kitted out with the right clothes," Peter said laughing.

"And," Max said sternly, "we're actually going to see one of the doctors on that list."

"Let me guess. An Aboriginal witchdoctor!" Peter laughed.

"Very droll," Max smiled.

"You've never visited here have you?" Peter asked "Do you think you, well we, are ready to head to the outback?" he said in a more serious tone.

"Look. I've got two INXS CDs, seen Neighbours once and hated it and like to gamble which about makes me a bloody citizen."

"Okay, okay," Peter laughed again feigning shock. They thought they would have a lot of planning ahead of them but the map showed the main highways which they guessed the coach companies would follow. Luckily the route was a fairly straightforward one. Dubbo, Broken Hill to the south, then straight up. Max scribbled notes onto the map and Peter lent his basic knowledge of Australia. Between them they produced a map with lots of scribbling on it. As they admired their handiwork Max stood up saying,

"We'd better find a travel agents or something." Peter nodded as Max popped a couple of mints into his mouth. They headed down the mall, Peter grinning and Max crunching. It wasn't long before they found a travel shop and were negotiating two economy tickets to Alice Springs. The agent hadn't heard of Napperby and Max thought it better not to labour the point. The bus left from the main city station at 3pm.

"You know what we need?" Peter said as they left the shop.

"An understanding God?" replied Max.

"And hats," said Peter, "we'll fry in the heat of the outback without hats and suntan lotion." Max spun around and shouted back to the girl behind the counter.

"Is there anywhere local to get a hat......cheap?" he added quickly. She smiled waving her hand to the left.

"Disposals store, across the street two blocks to the left."

The sun was still blazing as they left the mall and Max was glad Peter had mentioned protecting themselves from its wrath. '*Come to think of it,*' he thought as he passed people on the street, *'lots of these Aussies wear hats, stay covered up and have that pasty white colour of people that avoid the sun.'* As they reached the disposals store, the shop next door caught Max's eye. He gave the money to Peter and motioned that he should do the shopping.

"I'll meet you here in five minutes," he said quickly and darted into the shop next door. It was a large cluttered shop and there were two assistants behind the counter. One was probably the owner Max guessed, in his fifties and greying. The other was an acne-ridden teenager who leapt to attention from the magazine he was engrossed in as Max neared the counter.

"I wonder," Max began as he fumbled in his jeans' pocket, "if you have any of these in stock?" he said pulling out the bent bullet now attached to a number of miscellaneous keys. He dropped the bunch into the eager young man's hands and waited as he held it up to the light turning it over and over. After some umming and ahhing he reluctantly shook his head. This seemed to be the signal for the older man to walk over. He took the object of interest and scrutinised it through his half-rim glasses He raised his eyes to Max's and asked blankly.

"You're from Gun Monthly aren't you?" and before Max could answer, "I've heard your questions have got tougher. I got fourth best retailer three years ago you know." The last point was made with such pride that it prompted Max to pause and felt it would do no harm to humour him.

"Oh dear, I guess you have got me," he said trying to sound sincere. He shrugged then raised his eyebrows and looked back down at the bullet.

"Well?" he said with eager anticipation. "Which gun would this have come from?"

"Oh yes," the man said excitedly and with an air of confidence.

"It's a .22 cartridge from a series 4 Baretta. It will have been made in the USA between 1983 and 1992 as they have now been superseded by a newer version." Max jotted the details down on his notepad and had to admit that he was impressed. He felt fairly confident that the skinny man in front of him was spot on though he wouldn't know if he wasn't. As he looked up the two were grinning profusely at him.

"I'll just wander," he said awkwardly making a circular motion with his hands. The man nodded and the two quickly tried to look busy. Max wandered through rack upon rack of guns, crossbows and hunting accessories and pretended to pause and make notes. Shortly he reached the door and called out over his shoulder.

"I have a feeling that you'll do well this year," which was greeted with large grins and a pat on the back for the younger chap.

'What am I like?' Max thought as he bumped into Peter coming out of the other shop. Peter handed him the hat which was a little too small but nevertheless sat on his head quite well.

"To the station and a phone box," he said triumphantly and they headed off down the road at a brisk pace. Peter held out a number of blocks before his curiosity got the better of him. Max filled him in on his brief visit to the gun shop which prompted Peter to give him a mock telling off for having so much front. They got to the bus station with plenty of time to spare and squeezed into a phone booth with some difficulty. Max took some time to be sure about the number and checked the dialling codes. It rang quite a few times before it was picked up and it was evident why.

"This had better be bloody good!" the voice rasped harshly, "do you realise its barely four thirty!"

'Shit,' thought Max glancing at his watch, he hadn't remembered the time difference.

"Hi Andy. Sorry about the timing."

"Max?" the voice was confused but now very alert. "I thought you were dead?"

"Pretty close a couple of times," Max chuckled. "Sorry I can't tell you where I am but this is a transatlantic call and I'm pretty pressed for time."

"Sure," replied Andy who was now perched on the edge of the bed.

"I need you to check something," Max said pausing while Andy grabbed a pen and paper. He continued with all the detailed notes he had made half an hour earlier. Andy's voice was slow at the other end of the line.

"I can tell you that straight off, but you might not like it," he said and paused. "There's only one organisation that uses that type of Baretta and it ain't the boy scouts."

"Okay," said Max slowly.

"It's the Central Intelligence Agency," he said pausing again. "Is there anything I can do?" he asked solemnly. Max tried to sound calm but still rushed his goodbyes. He placed the receiver down slowly in an exaggerated manner and he and Peter stared at each other.

"CIA," they said simultaneously then, "Shit", Max and "Balls" Peter together. They both looked around, which was difficult as there wasn't much space inside the booth.

"Look, if they were here do you think that we still would be?" asked Max shaking. Peter forced a smile but neither of them felt comfortable walking to the bus or indeed once they were planted in their seats.

**** **** **** ****

The blinds were half-open and the spacious room was bathed in a misty haze that owed much to the clear dawn sky. There were two people by the bed. The closest to the window was a golden-haired woman who was fast asleep. Over her lap was a heavy check blanket and covering her feet leather moccasins with fluffy rims. *'Even fast asleep she looks tired,'* the man on the other side of the bed thought. Very few people (bar the man lying motionless between them) would have seen her pretty face without makeup. She had been there for two weeks now. There when he spoke his last words, there for the first operation, there for the tenth, there for the twenty-three times his bed lay empty, waiting to see if his body would return to fill it once more. He looked at the myriad of tubes that ran from the drips and machines and back at her. He had made sure that he had been there as much as his commitments would allow. Was his sympathy spurred on by the memory of his departed wife or from the fear that the man in front of him was only two years his senior. It was too quiet in the room. He hated the pressure the silence put on him to think. A dozen subjects worthy of his time fought to get to the surface but the feelings of sadness pushed them away with ease. The door opened very slightly letting in a shaft of light. He rose quietly from his chair and crossed to the door. As he closed it behind him he acknowledged the two young men either side and adjusted his eyes to the brightness of the corridor. Business called. It called today in the shape of an immaculately dressed lady with an equally immaculate, if somewhat fierce, short haircut.

"Good morning, Sir," she said, and as they walked down the corridor she added quietly, "We have come up against a bit of a problem." She hesitated a moment as she surveyed his heavily bloodshot eyes.

"Dr. Price will need another donor by Monday and London and Frankfurt have come up blank." She looked down at her clipboard waiting for his reply.

"Transfer someone," he said bluntly.

"I'm not sure I follow," she replied. She did, but for the record she wanted him to be explicit.

"Just get someone, anyone that fits the bill. Do I have to spell it out for you?" The last sentence had been a shouted whisper, menacingly spat out. She nodded and he felt a little guilty. After all it wasn't her fault. If she was hurt she didn't show it merely straightening and delivering a sharp salute.

"Yes Sir." The moral implications of his order reared their ugly head but he held them back. *'Anyway',* he thought *'I'm only following orders too. What the agency wants the agency gets.'* Still, if the man in there hadn't been his closest friend he would have told the precious agency to shove it. He wasn't afraid to be 'retired'. In fact, the idea had become more and more attractive over the past few weeks.

**** **** **** ****

The coach they had chosen, or rather had chosen them by virtue of being the cheapest, stood before them. Max checked twice that it was in fact theirs as the haphazard way it had been parked meant it could have been in either bay 15 or bay 16. The tell tale point that swung it was a piece of card with the words 'Alice Express' written in green felt tip that sat in pride of place in the windscreen in front of the steering wheel. Despite the scratches and the rust, there was a certain sturdiness about it that the new clean coaches lacked. They had fifteen minutes before it departed.

'That's if it starts,' Max thought. As they had no luggage, bar one small shoulder bag, they had time to wander and check

out the other passengers. In a forty-five seater bus twelve people seemed few, but as the driver explained most of the passengers would join in Sydney.

"It'll be like a Donegal pub during happy hour on St. Patrick's day," he grinned. Yes, their driver was of Irish descent and despite over twenty years of Aussie conditioning, still retained a broad Irish accent. The people on the bus, as Max and Peter inspected them, were a mixed bunch. Five were backpackers of varying description and nationalities. Two of them had more than likely been to Asia recently as flowing garments of coloured cotton covered most of their denim and worn footwear. The other three wore the more traditional creased and stained T-shirts. A middle-aged couple sat conservatively in the middle of the bus and an elderly couple right up at the front, as they invariably do. The last passenger didn't seem to fit in at all. He was a young priest who they later found out was on a visit to a number of Aboriginal settlements in the outback. He was in the row of seats opposite them, two thirds down the bus. Peter was around the same age as him and the two hit it off fairly quickly. The bus kicked into motion with a sound that few would have experienced, except those that had knocked a dozen tins of nails over in their shed. The driver guided the bus out of the garage accompanied by a low thumping noise from the engine. The elderly couple looked disturbed and the middle aged couple mildly worried. The backpackers were completely unmoved. Max and Peter were too occupied looking for suspicious people in the crowds and masses to take any notice either. It was only when the bus had left the city streets behind and was ambling down the highway that they sat back in their seats and relaxed a little. Peter looked at Max who he could sense was nervous. Actually he could hear his nervousness. He had crunched his way through two packets of mints in the last fifteen minutes. Behind them, one of the backpackers was listening to his Walkman so loud that either he had, or would soon have, a hearing problem. Max had glanced in his direction and scowled a couple of times. He was beginning to get wound up. Peter heard him utter something about relocating the offending stereo but Peter put his arm on the seat in front blocking Max's path to the aisle. Max was about to snap at him but was handed a pen and paper by the young priest. He had been watching the two with interest and guessed it was only a matter of time before Max lost his cool. Max forced a smile back and felt a little ashamed at his anger in front of a man of the cloth. He sat back down and wrote a few brief lines and handed the scrap to Peter who dutifully delivered it to the young man. He edited it on the way adding a 'please' and removing a few of the smaller more offensive words. The receiver of he note was in the middle of a sounding rendition of the subtle classic 'Bring your daughter to the slaughter' and was decidedly pissed off by the contents of the note, however justified. Peter had identified the originator and egged on by his mate he was going to 'teach the cheeky bastard a good lesson.'

"Oi you, note writer!" he baited from his battle position in the aisle at the back. Max got up past Peter and stood face to face with the young man. He walked forward and growled.

"Yes?" with his face a mere six inches from the lad's nose. In a few moments the taste for blood, the macho spur and manly bravado evaporated. Beads of sweat appeared on his shaved head as he examined his foe. No daylight passed him from the front of the coach so he was kinda large. The look on his face revealed that he wasn't having a very good day.

"I'm , er, sorry about the, erm, noise," he stammered.

"That's all right then," Max replied in the same deep growl and returned to his seat. The confrontation had a profound effect on the young man's music listening. The Walkman wasn't used at all for the remainder of the day. The young priest appeared pleased with the outcome and congratulated Max on his non-violent solution to the problem. Max closed his eyes and tried to sleep but his mind was racing. Eventually at around 2am with the highway rolling by outside the window, he fell into a deep sleep.

*** *** *** ***

Anders stepped off the plane. His eyes were hidden as ever behind those sunglasses. After him gingerly walked Easton. They had been flying on and off for 20 hours and the latter hadn't slept a wink. They had endured four dismal films, eight mediocre meals and a trio of irritating Scandinavians in front of them who managed between them to deplete most of the plane's 'free' alcohol stocks. Easton could now go to any North European beer festival and hold his head high as he was sure that at least two of their drinking songs were imprinted on his brain forever. It was close to midday and the airport at Newcastle was fairly quiet. For the sake of speed they had assumed the same identities as before and were kitted out in the same drab suits. As they passed through immigration, the officer paused as he examined their passports. As a precaution for each mission they were adorned with a visa for each continent and this surprised the man. He found it odd that such dull looking gentlemen would travel so much.

"You're doing a lot of travelling gentlemen," he said enquiringly.

"Yes we have a new medical discovery that we're very excited about," replied Easton with only a hint of enthusiasm.

The officer was about to enquire further when he noticed Easton's heavily bloodshot eyes. He smiled to himself as he stamped their visas in and thought, *'Bloody yanks, can't teach the buggers to leave the in-flight grog alone.'* They headed straight for the coffee lounge and sat at a table in the corner. Easton opened his case slowly to reveal his laptop and various attachments. Plugged into the side was a mobile phone and on this he dialled a long number and closed the case. They both ate a hearty breakfast. Easton had eggs, bacon, sausages and a plateful of toast with a large black coffee. Anders opted for muesli, herb bread and freshly squeezed orange juice. As he started on his third glass Easton moved his tray onto the next table and lifted the case back up in front of him once more. He opened the case and the screen told him that the data he had requested had been successfully transferred. The mini-printer sprung into motion. It was an annoying fact that they had to wait until they had come off the plane but the one time they had ignored the warnings the 737 they were on had developed 'technical problems' and had made a hurried landing.

"There's only seventeen travel agents in the whole town," he said slowly reading from the printout, "and, according to this only three sold pairs of tickets for cash in the past two days," he added a little surprised.

"Not exactly a booming travel industry," Anders agreed.

"Do you think they would be smart enough to buy the tickets separately?" Easton asked.

"Nah," Anders replied confidently, "but if the doubles don't work then we'll try the singles I suppose," he added. They took a cab from the airport into the city and it didn't take them long to find the right travel agent. It was the second on their list. Easton had no problem getting the information from the young lady there either as their two 'friends' were quite conspicuous. Besides, he was a handsome young American, even in such a dull grey suit. They were both smiling as they left the shop; Anders at the thought of catching up with his quarry and Easton at the prospect of a good night's sleep. A plane would get them to Alice Springs in a mere five hours so they didn't have to leave until the next morning.

**** **** **** ****

Supermodels Elle Macpherson and Claudia Schiffer had had their differences before but never over a man. The rift between them had grown so wide, the fall of their blooming café chain was rumoured to be around the corner. The flames had dulled a little the past week as the media circus had directed its attention elsewhere, but they were roaring now. Claudia had arrived at the luxurious Karma Lodge hotel with the aforementioned man for a fashion show only to find that Elle, one of his past loves, was staying a few doors down from them. He guessed that it had been done on purpose. Elle had held a candle for him that last year. It was a tragic scene really. He eased back into the big leather armchair and ordered another double scotch. Claudia was near the bar chatting briskly to a couple of beer-bellied media tycoons. She was wearing a daring white figure-hugging dress. She smiled at him one moment and threw evil stares in Elle's direction the next. She, in contrast, was in an excitingly short red dress that showed off those lovely legs. Little did Claudia know he had set up a secret meeting with Elle later that evening. His scotch arrived delivered by a beautiful blond waitress who smiled shyly at him. He sipped the drink casually.

'That's odd,' he thought, *'I can't remember Glenfiddich tasting of blackcurrant.'* He looked at the glass and sniffed. It smelt fine. Claudia smiled at him again.

'Ahh, the bliss of having two of the world's most beautiful women in the world fight over you,' he thought as he eased lower into the chair. The chattering was fairly loud but he thought he heard someone calling his name. He turned around and looked at the grey-haired man who seemed uncomfortable in his dinner jacket.

'He looks familiar. Oh bollocks,' he thought, *'Its my geography teacher, Mr Rawlins.'*

"Come on, what's the capital of Kenya? Well Jones?" The images became blurred and he caught one last glance of Claudia's smile.

Max's head felt heavy and his eyes sore as he opened them to a squint in the brightness. His back felt odd and he found he had slipped half way down in his seat. He opened his eyes a little wider and noticed Peter was not in the next seat but over with young priest. He was calling over to him. Max yawned and managed a barely audible grunt

"Yeah?"

"What's the capital of Kenya Max?" asked Peter for the third time. It was the last crossword clue left in Barry's newspaper.

"Nairobi." Max answered without thinking and reached for his hip flask. He took a swig. *'Shit,'* he thought, *'must get some more Scotch.'* It had run out the day before and Peter had filled it with blackcurrant cordial of all things. Max became aware that the coach was moving. It seemed smoother than before but probably because he had got used to its rumblings. He pulled back the small curtain and an arid landscape whizzed past the window. The earth was an orangey-yellow colour, sparsely populated with trees and shrubs that looked in desperate need of some water.

'How could anything possibly survive out here?' he wondered. There were a few animals on the horizon which Max took to be sheep.

"They're grey kangaroos," said Peter sitting back down next to him and smiling.

"We've seen loads of them. Barry says they're a pain in the ass - especially at night. He has to dodge them all the time. He even hit two on the last trip."

"I wondered what the bull bars were for on the front of the coach," said Max

"Yep, they call them 'Roo' bars over here," said Peter knowingly. Within the next hour they passed a lot of kangaroos, mostly hiding from the heat under trees and bushes. They would be in Broken Hill that evening to drop off and pick up more passengers. The bus was fairly full now, but not to the proportions that Barry had predicted. They stopped for lunch and fuel at one of those towns that seem to revolve around the petrol station. The heat hit them as they left the air-conditioning behind. Max's feet kicked up a lot of dust as they stretched their legs. There was a small general store which housed the bakers, the post-office and just about all the other services the place had to offer. It was owned by an elderly couple who both looked as strong as shire horses. They got a few provisions including lunch and more water this time as last time it had run out. They sat on a couple of boulders that were conveniently located under a tree a few yards down the road. They ate and chatted, mostly about what they thought of Australia. As he finished his last roll Max's tone turned serious.

"Pete, I think that when we get to Alice Springs we should go separate ways."

Peter tried to answer but Max carried on.

"Let me finish please. Before we got to here it was the IRA after me, us, and they don't operate outside the UK. This CIA thing is serious. We're damn lucky to have got this far in one piece."

"But they don't know where we're going," protested Peter.

"Yet," said Max, "and besides you've got plenty of background for a cracking story and when this is all over you can have the exclusive."

Peter waited and thought a little before replying.

"You've been thinking about saying that haven't you," he said eventually.

"Yeah," admitted Max. "It sound too corny?"

"A little," grinned Peter, "but it doesn't make a difference because I'm staying put, no arguments."

"Okay," said Max, "I would have felt guilty as hell had anything happened to you and I hadn't tried to persuade you to go," he said jokingly.

"Some persuasion," laughed Peter and mimicked Max's serious face, which set Max off laughing too. Their laughter carried quite a distance over the dry flat landscape and seemed to linger, for a moment anyway.

*** *** *** ***

Alice Springs was nothing like Easton had expected it. It was circled by a wonderful deep red mountain range and was, in fact, a vibrant town. The streets were full of tourists and hire cars sped around the roads. The first thing they did was to drive up to the top of Anzac hill near the centre of town. It gave them a view over the whole of the town and they got their bearings quickly. The saddest sight that greeted them at each corner was the aboriginal people in small groups. Most of them were clutching bottles or wine boxes and it was only mid morning. They looked for somewhere to have lunch with Easton hoping for a raw steak with a pile of fries and definitely no salad. He reluctantly followed his partner into a café on the corner of the street opposite the bus station and prepared himself for the worst. The town had health food fever, fuelled by the

Australian 'Year of Health' which had worked its way to the outback. It seemed only the aboriginal people had been left out, as the menu was dominated by pulses and vegetables.

Sam sat alone in the bus depot coffee shop. To the passer by, he was an average Joe reading his morning paper and listening to classical music on his Walkman. The loud music drowned the voices in his left earpiece.

"X1 - they have entered Marti's café and look like they are getting their lunch."

"X2 - my thoughts too. What do you think, a nice Kanga burger?"

"X1 - not funny X2."

Sam smiled. He did like working in this team, there was never a dull moment. Angie was kitted out as a young mum pushing a pram doing some window-shopping. That guise had been chosen due to the hoards of women with kids in town. It seemed to have a very migrant population. There were a couple of hours before the bus was due and it was just a matter of waiting. Sam bought another coffee and started to read the paper for the second time around.

The bus would be late, despite the fact that it was only an hour out of the town. The bus was at the side of the road and its passengers sat in the shade it created. Barry the driver was underneath fighting with a spanner and jack to get two of the wheels off that had decided to give up and burst on the last bend. To make matters worse, the air-conditioning had packed up two hours earlier. The temperature inside the bus had climbed to a very uncomfortable 50°c. It wasn't too much cooler outside but at least there was a breeze. What really pissed him off was that his Guiness supply for that evening was the latest casualty of the heat. Two cans had already split and the rest had been hurriedly moved from behind his seat to under the bus in the shade with him. He cursed aloud as he heard another pop and spring a leak. His hands were oily and sweaty and the bolts were proving pretty stubborn.

Peter and the young priest had decided the enforced stop was the ideal opportunity to explore the nearby 'bush'. Despite the heat and looking pretty daft in his hat, Max felt obliged to join them and tagged along. Everything was so red. The shrubs that were speckled around looked almost wiry. The sky was so blue and even through sunglasses it was very bright. Peter pointed out the charred earth and rocks, which, he explained, were tell-tale signs of a recent bush-fire. It amazed Max that the landscape they stood in had recently been ravaged by fire. The plants had simply taken it as par for the course and had begun to grow back slowly. As they continued further down the road they looked eagerly for signs of wildlife. They didn't have to wait long as they approached a dead kangaroo by the side of the road. Sitting astride the animal that had probably been hit by a truck was a magnificent wedge-tailed eagle. They had seen a few from the bus but it was only when they were within twenty feet that they realised the real size of these birds. Rather than scare it off they diverted off the road and headed toward a patch of greenery that Peter had spotted.

Barry hadn't struggled for too long before offers of help started coming thick and fast. The more able-bodied people's opinion seemed to be that any way to get the heap moving again quickly should be employed. There was no such luck with the air-conditioning. Barry tinkered with it for about five minutes while two of the lads put the finishing touches to the second wheel. He knew his limits though and decided to leave it. There was a feeble cheer from the mass of bodies sprawled next to the bus as he announced with a cheeky Irish grin that the journey could continue. He was now down to only four cans of Guiness, which didn't put him in the best of moods getting back to his seat. He started to count the passengers on but gave up as they piled on too quickly. The ubiquitous question.

"Are we all here?" was shouted backwards which received a chorus of impatient Yes's and that was good enough for him.

The young priest paused in the middle of his examination of the cluster of flowers in front of him and looked up puzzled.

"Isn't that the bus's engine?" he said slowly. All three of them listened carefully and realised they must have strayed further away then they had thought.

"I hope that means he's testing the air-conditioning," said Peter as he quickened his step.

"He wouldn't leave us here surely, would he?" said the young priest now breaking into a run. Max didn't contribute to the conversation as running fast took all his energy and breath. Judging by the slow speed he went at, he didn't have much of either. He quickly lost ground to his companions and very soon lost sight of them as they disappeared over a ridge. Max slowed to a walk puffing heavily. It was no good, the heat was just too much for a man of his age. He groaned as he reached the top of the ridge holding his side with sweat pouring down his face. The sight that greeted him didn't exactly cheer him up either. The two young men stood staring blankly at the horizon where the only evidence of their bus was a dust cloud in the distance.

"Oh great," Max managed to get out before collapsing onto a rock.

"Erm, at least we've got our bag," said Peter holding it up sheepishly. It dawned on him that Father Vernon's belongings were probably still on the bus and he blushed deeply. The young priest saw this and smiled.

"Oh, mine were sent on a few days ago. I too only have what I am carrying."

Max tried to be angry but he was too exhausted. Peter was waiting for an outburst but was surprised when Max got up and started walking. The other two shrugged and looked at Max who turned and said.

"Look it's 2pm and Barry said we were around an hour from the town. I reckon that means around 50km. We're bound to find a house with a phone inside a couple of hours," he said with surprising optimism. They were both impressed and followed him down the road. They were just far enough behind him not to hear him swearing under his breath.

**** **** **** ****

Sam, Angie and Tom were used to waiting. They had once waited two days to snare a Chilean diplomat who was trying to bribe a CIA agent. They had got him and this would be a walk in the park in comparison. They had now changed about. Sam and Tom had switched places courtesy of a visit to the gents. Tom emerged with the Walkman and a copy of Business Week. The music this time was the new album from Harry Connick Junior. Angie had ducked into a nearby shopping mall within reach of the bus station. Inside Marti's café, Anders and Easton were on their fourth round of coffee. Anders was on the de-caf naturally. From where he sat, he could see the road in toward the bus station and every time a coach or bus came along it he would switch the glasses he was wearing to long-sight and check the bus details.

'*Marvellous,*' thought Easton, '*the Agency can develop the technology to incorporate 16 times magnification in a pair of normal sunglasses, but I can't lay my hands on a decent steak.*' He looked down at the remains of cauliflower cheese and fishbake and grimaced.

"OK lets make a move," said Anders quietly and got up from the table leaving the money for the meal (no tip) on his napkin. They walked across the road to the bus station and Angie and Sam moved in closer. Anders walked into the bus café while Easton went to the bay adjoining and sat beside a pregnant woman holding a baby. He hid his face behind a magazine and watched as a tired and pissed off Barry finally brought the bus to rest in the bay. The people rolled off in a ramshackle mass looking worn. He was very surprised when the last person staggered off and Max and Peter were nowhere to be seen. He decided quickly that the driver would certainly know where they had got off. Maybe they had underestimated them again. Lulled into a false sense of security by the easy to trace tickets they'd fallen for one of the oldest tricks in the book. They were probably thousands of miles away by now.

"Excuse me," he said to Barry who was collecting his bag and cherished, if somewhat depleted, Guiness stock.

"Yes?" he replied tersely.

"My two friends were supposed to be on this bus. Both pommes. One 6ft tall and stocky with dark hair. The other shorter."

"Yes?" Barry was tired, fed up and needed a drink.

"Well they didn't get off the bus just now," Easton said slowly.

"Listen pal," Barry said unsympathetically, "Your mates were on this bus an hour ago. I'm the driver, not their bleeding mother. If they've disappeared that's their business. I'm off for a pint." With that he headed off for the nearest pub. Easton forced a smile. So they were coming here, just took the precaution of switching transport before they got into town. He found Anders and filled him in on the developments. They chatted for a moment and reverted to their backup plan (which they had just made).

"X2 - looks like they screwed it up again."

"X1 - nice choice of phrase X2," Angie laughed.

"Looks like they are dealing with two pretty smart cookies."

Max didn't feel like a smart cookie. He was uncomfortable and hot. Ah yes, and he must remember to add sheep after fish on his list of things he didn't like. So far in the back of this truck, two had decided to lunch on his shirt and one had dumped on his foot. He wished the kind farmer who had stopped to pick up the three struggling walkers hadn't had two dogs which occupied the front seats. He was too tired to chat avidly like Peter and Padre over there. Max kept forgetting the young priest's name and Padre seemed much more appropriate. Max guessed they had walked around 5km before they had been picked up (it was actually a little over 2km) and they had been eager to jump in the back, albeit with around thirty sheep. What really pissed him off was that they seemed to stare at him before they tried to eat his clothing. They had chosen their seating positions very carefully, for obvious reason. This meant that Max had ended up on the other side of the truck. His eyelids were heavy and he closed them to rest for a moment. Despite the bumpy ride and noisy co-passengers he drifted off.

Angie and Sam kept a long-distance eye over Easton and Anders as the two went around the town visiting all the inns, hotels and hostels in a methodical way and finally ended up at their own, The Melrose. Their three shadows checked in across the road.

The farmer lived on the outskirts of town and he dropped them off before he turned down the side-road. Padre offered to buy them a drink and they both heartily accepted. It was only a short walk and they were through the door of his hotel within ten minutes. He suggested that they might find a room there too, which sounded like a good idea. They all headed toward the reception in their little group and rang the small bell. The clean-cut young man behind the counter gave them a warm smile.

"What can I do for you fellas?" he said.

"I have a room booked under Father Vernon McDade and these two gentlemen would also like a roof over their heads," said Padre.

"I'm sure we can manage that Father, I'll just get the manager for you," he replied and disappeared. In a moment he was replaced by a man with more waist and less hair than his younger colleague.

"Good evening Father, we've been expecting you. Your luggage arrived yesterday," he said with due reverence and paused whilst looking at Max and Peter.

"Are these two gentlemen with you?" he asked looking a bit puzzled.

"They certainly are," he beamed.

"Well then, there must have been some mistake," he said and added with a whisper,

"I had two fellows in here about an hour ago looking for two guys travelling by themselves. Their descriptions of these two are spot on, but they reckoned you guys were very dodgy characters."

Max swallowed hard.

"Oh man," he said "not those two bozos again," looking at Peter he added chuckling,

"I wonder what they pretended to be this time, CIA, FBI, or MI5," he laughed sourly.

"Oh, they didn't say," said the landlord quickly to make sure they didn't realise he'd fallen for the CIA trick.

"So who are these guys then?" he asked. Max was on a roll now and was waiting for that question.

"Well, about five years ago me and Pete worked in the tax fraud office and we busted those two guys for a time-share scam. They conned hundreds of pensioners out of their life savings," he said, looking disgusted.

"The bastards only got three years and they were out in two. They've been after us ever since," Max added shaking his head.

"Bastards," echoed the landlord. "And they had the cheek to ask me to phone them if you came in here. They slipped me twenty bucks for my trouble too."

Max thought for a moment then whispered.

"Would you mind helping us put one over on them?"

"Nothing would give me greater pleasure mate," he said enthusiastically.

"OK," Max continued, "I'll need pen and paper, a pair of binoculars, and of course a phone."

The landlord grinned. "No worries."

Easton and Anders were sitting in their room reading their respective papers. As ever there was a lack of conversation and it was quiet when the phone rang. Anders answered it with a simple

"Yes?"

"Hiya mate. Its Jack from the Duke here. You know those two guys you're looking for?"

"Yes?" Anders said flatly.

"Well, they came here about twenty minutes ago and headed off to the Rock Lodge out on Valley Road for the night."

"OK where is that?" Anders was getting excited but didn't let it show in his voice.

"It's the first road off the Central Square. How about the rest of the money?" he added, trying to sound greedy.

"You'll get it," Anders assured him, "Just as soon as we get them." He put down the phone and tossed the hire car keys to Easton.

"You can always rely on people's greed," he grinned.

"As sweet as a possum in a pie," said the landlord after he put the phone down softly. Max, Peter and Padre all smiled and, binoculars in hand, went up the stairs to the roof. As they watched Valley Road Max noted the license plate of a red saloon which sped down the road. "Part two," he said as he walked back down the stairs. He went to the phone behind the counter with the others crowded around him. He dialled and a voice at the other end said, "Hello, police service, how can I help you?" In his best Scottish accent Max said, "Ah, thank god. Some sassanach has stolen ma hire car under ma nose. The bastards waved their guns at me as they drove off," he sounded very flustered.

"OK Sir, please calm down. Where are you phoning from and what's your name?" she asked slowly.

"I'm in the Duke. I ran across the road to phone. Me name's Angus McDougal, but they'll get away m'girl," he said sounding panicked.

"Yes OK sir, what's the registration and which direction did they go?" she said calmly.

"Oh yes, sorry, its one of those red Hertz things. UMX-401, a Holden I think."

"And the direction?" she asked again.

"Oh yes, Valley Road," Max replied.

"Don't worry Sir, we'll do our best. You just stay put and we'll get them all right," she said reassuringly.

"Thanks I will," Max said and put the phone down and grinned like a Cheshire cat.

'By the time they get out of that one we'll be well out of here.'

He thanked the landlord who seemed to be as happy with the success of the phone call as Max himself.

Anders and Easton reached the T junction at the end of Valley Road. They stopped the car and were puzzled. It was only a short road and there had only been one hotel on it and that was 'The Pines'.

"Shit," exclaimed Eaton slamming his hands on the steering wheel. He pointed to the left and Anders looked back to see a large boulder with a sheet of paper stuck to it. Anders got out calmly and returned with the piece of paper and read its contents aloud.

"I'm sorry I can't come to the rock right now. Please wait for the tones, leave a message and I'll get back to you, Max." He looked at Easton who forced a smile.

"OK, we've been done. But what did he mean by the tones?" He said inquisitively. Anders didn't need to answer as they heard the police siren behind them and saw the flashing lights. Moments later a loud hailer boomed,"

"Throw your weapons out of the windows and come out of the car with your hands behind your head, then down on your knees."

"Shit," said Easton as he tossed his .35 and Anders' Baretta out of the window. They followed the instructions to the letter and as they kneeled side by side, Easton whispered.

"Have you got your ID?"

"Nope," Anders replied. "Mine's in the motel too. But don't worry, I'll sort out these country hicks."

"X1 - this has got to be a first. Our two friends have only been arrested!"

"X2 - yep, did you get close enough to see them on their knees and trussed up in cuffs?"

"X1 - no X2, but I'm sure it was a real Kodak moment."

"X2 - I guess we'll have to stake out the police station now," Tom laughed.

"X1 - shame we can't interfere and get them out isn't it."

"X2 - yeah real shame."

"X1 - they'll be out by the morning if they're nice to the locals. Now you two boys get some shut eye. I'll cover the station," said Angie.

"X2 - no arguments from me. Nighty night"

"Hicks eh?" said Easton quietly as he ran his fingers up and down the bars of their cell. Anders ignored him and instead focused his attention on the sergeant sitting at his desk twenty feet away.

"Hey, Sarge," he said loudly.

"You realise this will be a major international incident if these two felons escape?"

"Oh good," said the round sergeant without lifting his eyes from his magazine.

"My wife works for the local paper. They've been painfully short of 'major international incidents' in the last few months," he said grinning.

"If you'll just retrieve our IDs from our motel you can verify them within the hour," Anders growled.

"Sure. I'll just ring Judge Molten and ask him to pop to the court buildings and whip up a warrant," he said picking up the phone.

"Wait a minute!" he said in mock surprise in mid-dial.

"It's 1 am (looking at his watch) and the judge'll be asleep. Perhaps I'd better not," he said putting he phone back down and chuckling.

"Listen, you'll lose you're job if you don't sort this out, and damn quick. You can be sure of that," Anders shouted.

"All I can be sure of," the sergeant replied still grinning, "Is if I get the old judge out of his bed in the middle of the night I'll be out of here so fast my ass will land halfway across the street," he laughed again. Anders lay back down on his bunk. He was really, really pissed now. No quick death for that bastard Jones now, oh no. He'd rip him to pieces, starting with his head. Easton looked up as a young cop entered the room. He pointed at them and whispered something to the sergeant who burst out laughing. Anders buried his head under his pillow and Easton let out a deep sigh.

'This is going to be a long night,' he thought.

**** **** **** ****

Max and Peter got up early. After quick showers they stepped out into the morning sun. There was a bite in the air and not a cloud in the sky. It was going to be a glorious day. Their walk was only going to be a short one but Max still pulled the scribbled map from his pocket. One of their drinking partners the night before ran a 4WD hire place and had drawn them a map to it. Prompted by the landlord and the thirteen cans of VB he'd consumed, he'd offered them a free jeep for their visit to the outback. They quickly accepted, as their funds were pretty low. They found the yard easily.

"Tim's 4 Wheels" proclaimed the big red sign and below it a yard full of shiny Suzukis. In the middle of said yard was an office, or badly erected shed depending on your architectural persuasion. They both knocked on the door. No answer. Max knocked again much louder.

"Coming," came the muffled answer, then a bang (knee on desk) a quiet yelp and a few choice words describing the offending desk. The door opened and a bleary-eyed face greeted them with a big grin.

"Morning fellas," he said as cheerfully as he could muster. Judging by the look of him, his morning had been anything but good thus far. He honourably met his offer of the night before, which he remembered only vaguely. Max drove the jeep out of the yard and headed off down a back street. They were careful to avoid the area that housed the police station and within twenty minutes they were out on the highway, heading Northwest. Peter turned out to be a pretty good 'map man' and Max was content for him to issue directions as and when. Tim had reckoned on them taking around four hours to reach where they were going, with the assumption that they didn't get lost. He'd given them a short lecture about driving in the outback and Max had been very attentive. He'd seen the dents in their coach and sat through a number of Barry's 'disaster' stories. Peter was fascinated by the revelation that there were hundreds of thousands of camels in Australia.

"On account of the bloody big deserts," Tim had said. Very soon the heat of the day was upon them and they were glad of the air-conditioning, however simple. They were undoubtedly driving the oldest jeep from the lot and it had obviously seen more countryside than they had. Their field of vision was that much greater than it had been on the coach, which pushed home just how dusty, barren and orange the landscape was. They had only come across a few vehicles since leaving Alice behind but now in front of them was a line of traffic.

"Must be one of those 'road trains' up ahead that Tim mentioned," said Max and looked up the line of half a dozen cars and trucks ahead. He was quite right. There was a sixteen-wheeler with three trailers attached to it. Some cars had already passed it but those without a death-wish were waiting patiently for a long stretch of straight road. Max decided not to push his luck and after ten minutes followed the stream of traffic around the obstacle and the road quickly became quiet again. Max drove for another hour and then Peter took over. By the time they decided to have lunch they were only 1½ hours from Napperby. Once the engine was off it was lovely and peaceful. They had stopped in a parking area off the highway and sat with their backs to the jeep's wheels in the limited shade that the high sun gave. Another hastily prepared lunch from their bag - cold pies from the hotel the previous evening. Still, the lack of vitamins and minerals and a balanced diet are not usually high on the priority list of people evading the clutches of the CIA. They ate heartily and drank what seemed like endless cups of water.

"Just another few hours and you'll have the answers you need," said Peter as he leaned back on the wheel. Max sighed.

"I'm not sure he'll know, and if he does I'm not sure I'll want to know," he said sullenly. It had dawned on him as Peter said those words that he was pinning his hopes, and perhaps his life, on the next few hours.

When the cell doors had been opened hurriedly neither of them had said a thing. They picked up their Ids from the sergeant's desk and walked straight out of the front door into the sunshine. They hadn't acknowledged the chief inspector's presence at all but now, an hour later, they were back to make up for that. Anders stood opposite the chief, only a desk between them. Even before he opened his mouth the chief felt intimidated. His hands were on his hips, his jacket open and the butt of his Baretta jutting out. The chief held his palms up and said humbly, "What can I say gentlemen?"

"How about, 'Jeez we're buttheads, sorry about the fuck-up'," Easton sneered.

The chief was a little taken aback but was locked in Anders' piercing stare.

"Sit down Chief," Anders said calmly. Like an obedient puppy he did just that. Anders placed his hands on the desk and leaned forward.

"I won't waste my time with recriminations. My department will see to that," he paused for effect, then continued. "Firstly I want this whole fiasco kept watertight. If any of this gets to the press I will hold you personally responsible."

The chief nodded.

"Second, all your men are to be issued with photos of these two. In the unlikely event that they come back here, I want them rounded up and held until we come and take them off your hands."

The chief nodded again.

"And finally, I'd like a helicopter fully fuelled here inside half an hour. No pilot."

The last request surprised Easton. He wouldn't admit it but he was impressed. The chief was about to object but Anders' relentless stare reminded him that he was in no position to bargain. He nodded again and turned to the sergeant passing on the orders with a wave of his hand. The officer shot out of the room glad to get out of there. In a little under an hour, Anders and Easton were walking toward a helicopter in the middle of a small field three blocks down from the police station. Anders was an experienced pilot, having flown all manner of 'copters in Korea and Vietnam and on a number of assignments for the agency. Easton had only flown with him once and that had been pretty frightening. At least this time it was daylight and they were the ones that were armed. They climbed into the front seats and Anders laid the .22 rifle they had commandeered behind the seat. It was an odd looking whirlybird. It used to be a crop sprayer in its first life but had been converted for use on sightseeing tours. Whoever had done it had extended its range so they had plenty of fuel. Anders lifted the bird off the ground ten feet, dipped the front and sped off. The gust knocked a number of dustbins over and the sergeant's hat flew off over a fence. Easton glanced back and smiled, then crossed his fingers.

**** **** **** ****

They asked in the 'town' about the doctor's house and the deli owner directed them back along the road they had travelled down. The only evidence that the house was in fact there, was a rusted mailbox that stood alone about ten feet off the road. The name on the box matched, so they headed off the bitumen in search of the house. It was two o'clock and it was hot. The jeep was so covered in dust it looked like a moving sand dune. They drove another three or so kilometres and Max realised why the mailbox was on the road.

"How often do you think the post gets out here?" he asked.

"If they're lucky twice, but I reckon once a week," replied Peter, who was busy watching the bush for bird-life. There were so many fantastic birds in the countryside here, parakeets of all colours and patterns. *'Even the crows here are pretty,'* Peter thought, as an orange and grey one darted past his window. As Max drove over the next ridge they saw the house. They were both surprised by its simplicity. A house surrounded by so much land would have been much grander in England. But then Max supposed the little two bedroomed, corrugated iron roofed house probably cost more than the barren land it sat on. By the time they rolled up to the front porch a grey-haired man was standing out on it. He'd probably seen the dust cloud from a couple of miles away. A large Alsatian sat obediently by his side. Max had a healthy respect for well-trained dogs. His left buttock still bore the scars of his childhood neighbours' dog's teeth, a huge German Shepherd that had thwarted a ball-retrieving trip one Sunday morning. They got out of the jeep and walked toward the house stopping a respectful twenty feet from the steps.

"Good afternoon, Sir," said Max cheerfully.

"Good afternoon," replied the doctor and added, "Insurance or Real Estate?"

Max quickly realised the mistake and laughed.

"Neither sir. My name is Max Jones and I would like to ask you a few questions that you may be the only one to answer," he said smiling.

"I doubt it," said the doctor, "unless the questions are 'what did you have for breakfast?' and 'how much milk have you got left in the fridge?'" He grinned

"Besides, I'm retired and according to local opinion I'm an eccentric old man."

"That's fine with me," Max said, "I don't have too many options and you really are my only chance." The doctor sensed the urgency in Max's voice and smiled.

"Well, you're probably in deep shit then, but I guess you can come in for a cup of tea," he laughed. They followed the doctor into the house taking great care that they didn't bring the outside in with them. Once inside Max and Peter felt they were walking around a mini-museum. They both gazed around at the fascinating objects that lined the walls, shelves and other surfaces of the living room. Max was captivated by the fireplace, which was gorgeous marble and by the portrait above it. The woman was stunningly beautiful and the picture looked a good forty years old. Time had not altered the smile and warm eyes that kept watch over the room.

"The kettle is on gentlemen, please do make yourselves at home," the doctor called from the kitchen. Max and Peter sat down on the couch which was a deep green with highly polished mahogany arms. It too had a feeling about it of being decades old. Max's eyes wandered past the portrait to the iron gas lamps that sat either side of it. He wondered if they were in fact functional, as he could not see any other forms of lighting in the room. Peter's eyes fell on the bookcase, which at one end held all medical journals and the other, classical fiction. 'Far From The Madding Crowd - Thomas Hardy' nestled amongst rows of Dickens and Jules Verne. Further on lay the works of Plato, Lenin and a host of other philosophers. Many of them large leather bound volumes that looked a delight to read. In front of the bookshelves was a small table with a chess-set mid-game. He studied it briefly and decided that white just had the upper hand. The back wall was full of certificates and diplomas all in beautiful script. Many were in German though the ones to the right were in English. The doctor emerged from behind a stately grandfather clock that sat next to the door to the kitchen.

He was carrying a silver tray with china teacups, saucers and a jug of milk jostling for space with an ornately detailed teapot. He laid it down on the table in front of them and sat down in an armchair.

"I'm afraid I'm out of Earl Grey, so normal tea will be OK I trust?" he said. It was a rhetorical question but Max still said, "Great". He was trying to relax a little and it wasn't working very well. They drank the tea and made small talk, mostly about the house and its contents. The lady in the picture was his late wife as Max had suspected. The gas lamps were real as there was no electricity in the house at all yet. He planned to have solar power in by the end of the year. Max finished his second cup of tea and sat back into his seat. The other two were still drinking, of course, and he decided that now was the time for serious talking.

"My first question doctor is this," he paused, "are you familiar with the fluid Panvidyxcil?" he said looking anxiously at their host.

"Yes, it is a cerebral fluid substitute. I have come across it a number of times during my research," replied the doctor. Max sighed with relief. He had found someone who knew what he was talking about.

"Why would someone use it?" he asked.

"Well, the only application it has is to keep brain tissue in a state of suspension long enough for experts to examine the cells in an 'alive' state. Its very useful in analysing cancerous patients to determine in the last few hours the course the cancer took."

"How long could the tissue be kept in that state?" Max asked slowly

"That's irrelevant really," replied the doctor who was curious as to where this was leading.

"Why?" asked Max.

"Simple. If you left the cells with cancer/disease for more than, say 48 hours they would have changed beyond measure."

"How about healthy tissue, for say, transplants?" The doctor was very curious now.

"Firstly, the cost of storing the tissue in a healthy state for the maximum of around sixty hours would be very costly. Secondly, the chances of matching compatible tissues is around one in fifty. Thirdly, the tissue would have to be extracted within minutes of death. Difficult in itself."

"Unless of course the patient is already in hospital," Max interrupted.

"I suppose so," agreed the doctor.

"Next, in around 75% of cases death itself renders all the tissue useless. Finally," he said slowly, "such a tissue transplant is highly unlikely to be very effective. So far in such operations patients' bodies initially accept the tissue but within a few weeks it is rejected and you are back to square one." Max thought about this for a moment.

"So, it would be possible to keep such a patient alive indefinitely if you were able to line up enough donors?" he asked.

"Technically yes. For the reasons I have outlined, practically no."

"What if you turned some of the odds back in your favour?" Max said solemnly.

"Hmm" the doctor thought. "The only factor you could physically influence..." he paused and cast a concerned look at Max.

"Would be to remove the tissue before the patient is actually dead," Max said slowly. He went on to explain piece by piece the events at the hospital and the records he had kept.

"These people must be stopped," the doctor said in a disgusted tone as Max finished.

"Whatever you need from me you've got it," he said earnestly.

"Thank you doctor," Max said, and took out pen and paper and began to write.

'Not a patch on a Hewey,' Anders thought as he sliced through the clear blue sky and kept his eyes glued to the horizon. Many memories of the two conflicts in which he had fought were painful, but they were more or less held back by better images - skimming the treetops and hovering over the lakes collecting his precious human cargo from the jaws of danger. Easton looked away from the stunning scenery to look at Anders' face and saw his past glories being relived. He was too young to have been part of the wars his partner had been in, except as an indirect casualty. His father had made it back from Vietnam and had been altered by its horrors. He seemed all right at first but then came the screams in the night, the mood-swings and the erratic temper. He didn't like to guess what was going on inside Anders' head. The agency was the natural choice for him. Easton turned his eyes back to the scenery. They would be there in half an hour from now. It would be close as to whether they would be in time.

**** **** **** ****

Max stopped the jeep at the end of the doctor's drive and thought for a moment.

"It's right back to Alice Springs, Max," Peter said. He was surprised Max had forgotten the way back. *'Still, he has a lot on his mind'* he thought. Max smiled briefly and pulled out left onto the road.

"North to Darwin," he said quietly.

"OK," said Peter trying to sound enthusiastic. Max had been solemn ever since they had left the doctor's front door.

"I suppose Tim can arrange for someone to pick up the jeep from there," he said.

"But I'm sure you thought of that," he added as an afterthought. Max hadn't. He was grappling with his next problem. Now he had the information he wanted, what the hell was he going to do with it?

It was about ten minutes after they turned off left that a large red helicopter flew low over the doctor's house. With no sign of the jeep they were looking for they headed back to the road and Anders brought the chopper to rest by the road a good 100 yards from the post-box and leapt out.

'You won't get away that easily,' he thought as he crouched over the tracks leading into the road. As he suspected one of the sets of tracks led out to the left.

'Got him,' he grinned as he walked casually back to the helicopter. The road in that direction (according to the map) ran plenty long enough to catch them up. The chopper rose off the

ground sending dust flying once more and sped off in a straight line above the road.

Peter was driving now. Max had found he couldn't concentrate and think at the same time. Had he known of the impending danger perhaps he would have had his foot to the floor but he was cautious as ever and respectful of the harshness of the road conditions. Max's hard thinking wasn't getting him anywhere and he decided he'd wait until that evening. A good meal and a couple of whiskeys would get the grey matter moving again.

Anders would normally be holding the rifle. On this occasion he had no choice but to let Easton have the honours. Easton was no slouch but he had seen Anders hit targets that he could barely see himself. They could see the jeep now and Easton loaded the rifle and checked the sights.

"Remember, just take out the wheels," Anders said slowly.

"I know," replied Easton, "and if the crash doesn't kill them then we'll have two prisoners."

'Two corpses either way,' thought Anders and started his descent.

"Oh look," said Peter. "A helicopter way out here," he smiled as he saw the speck get larger in his rear view mirror. Max wasn't listening properly but at the word helicopter he perked up.

"A what?" he said.

"Helicopter," Peter repeated and pointed over his shoulder. Max spun round and saw the quickly descending 'copter. He turned back telling himself not to be so silly. Where would they have got a helicopter from? He chuckled to himself and leant forward to turn on the radio.

"Now!" shouted Anders and Easton squeezed the trigger hard. His face was being blown about and was sure he'd missed.

The back window shattered with a crash and both Max and Peter let out unintelligible screams. Peter somehow managed to keep the jeep on the road and Max cursed himself vowing that from now on he would be a paranoid bastard.

"Keep weaving left and right," he shouted over to Peter. The noise from the road had increased due to the lack of a back window but *'he needn't have shouted,'* thought Peter. He then realised that worrying about being shouted at whilst being shot at was rather stupid.

Easton re-loaded the rifle and prepared to shoot again. He'd actually fired the second shot well wide. He wasn't being helped by Anders in his excitement calling him a 'Bloody Amateur'. He elected to aim for the front wheels this time but instead hit the bonnet. It turned out to be close enough.

Steam gushed out in front of him and made Peter's job of driving near impossible. They veered off the road to the right straight through a bush and down into a shallow river. They probably would have stopped there had the river not been dried up for many years. The jeep rapidly found its way out the other side.

"Tree!" yelled Max as another bullet thudded into the back of the jeep. Peter turned hard right and missed the tree but hit the wall behind it side on. The jeep flipped over and crashed onto its roof.

Easton had popped a few more shots as the jeep had made its way through the bush.

"Bingo!" shouted Anders gleefully as he saw the upturned jeep. He grinned as he noticed it sitting in the middle of a flower bed. As they swooped toward the ramshackle dwelling Easton saw a figure emerging.

'I bet he's pissed,' Anders thought. Another couple of seconds closer and Anders saw the figure raise his arms and before he could bank away fragments ripped through the 'copter sending it into a dive.

"No-one messes my cacti," shouted the man holding the shotgun and shaking his fist at the sky. As he turned and walked toward the jeep he saw that a couple of the wheels were still spinning.

"Urggh," Max grunted as he shifted in his seat. Well one thing was for sure, he was alive. His throbbing leg told him as much. *'Pete?'* he thought and anxiously turned his head, painful in itself, and called out his name.

"Pete." Peter opened one eye and curled up one side of his mouth at the same time.

"We alive then?" he asked sounding surprised.

"Yep, and upside down too," Max replied in a strained voice. He moved again which was a bad move as he slid down a foot or so, just enough to hit his head on the roof (currently doing a pretty good job as a floor).

"Ouch," he groaned and Peter bit his lip to stop himself laughing. Both windows had smashed in the crash and dust blew in and into Max's open eyes.

'That's all I need,' Max thought as he squinted and rubbed his eyes. As he opened them and looked across at Peter he let out a loud 'EEEK' and did his best to jump backward. All this in fact achieved was to rock the jeep and cause him to slip further out of his seat so his head was almost flat on the roof. The cause of his alarm was a dark face with a big grin that had appeared at Peter's window.

"G'day fellas," the man said cheerfully. "You do realise you are trespassing," he said in a serious tone and then laughed.

"Sorry about the wall," Peter said quickly.

"Oh screw the wall. I'm more worried about yer mate's leg there," he said pointing at Max's jeans that were blood-soaked below the knee. He opened Peter's door and helped him out and then they both tried to free Max. His door however had been wedged closed by the impact.

"Any time before Christmas," Max said loudly.

"Oh, a pomme with a sense of humour," laughed the man. "I'll just get a crowbar," he added and headed to the house. Within a few minutes Max was out, lying in the shade with his bloody leg in the air. It was propped up on an empty beer carton and his jeans cut away to reveal a deep gash with excellent scar potential.

"I'll need to stitch it, OK?" the man said matter-of-factly.

"You a doctor?" Max asked hopefully.

"You got a choice?" came the short reply.

"Anaesthetic?" Max smiled.

"My name's Mulwi and you see that log over there?" Max nodded "That's the only anaesthetic you'll get here."

"I'll pass thanks," laughed Max holding his hands up. "Got any Scotch?" he asked as an afterthought.

"Whiskey. Now you're talking like an Aussie. Sure." Mulwi got up and returned with a well-drained bottle that still had a dozen gulps left in it. Max knocked it straight back and gritted his teeth. As the needle was being held over the man's cigarette lighter Max closed his eyes. Despite the numbness of the leg the pain was intense but he was too proud to show it and didn't utter a sound until the last stitch went in. Mulwi was impressed with the big man's bravery and as he tied the stitch off he leaned down and whispered in his ear.

"You're supposed to scream you stupid pomme." Max laughed as he opened his eyes and saw that it was all over. Mulwi ran a bandage over the wound and Max extended his hand and thanked the tall man. Peter had watched quietly and decided to ask about what had been worrying him. He'd half been expecting their armed pursuers to leap out any moment.

"Did you see where the helicopter went?" he asked.

"They crashed somewhere over that ridge," Mulwi replied pointing out to their left.

"Crashed?" repeated Max.

"Yes, with a little help from my shotgun," Mulwi said proudly pointing to an ancient looking device which was leaning against a tree. It looked like a cross between a bugle and a Winchester.

"Why did you shoot at them?" asked Peter amazed.

"They shot at me first," Mulwi replied pointing at a bullet hole above the door.

"And besides, they ruined my cacti," he added turning to where the jeep lay amongst a once beautiful bed of cacti.

"I didn't hear an explosion though," Mulwi said jumping to his feet and heading off in the direction of the 'crash'. Peter and Max followed tentatively. Mulwi had picked up his shotgun and was reloading it from a pouch underneath his T-shirt as he walked. Max winced a little from the pain but his leg wasn't too bad all things considered. As they reached the peak of the ridge they saw a clump of Boab trees, one of which had the remains of a helicopter entwined in its branches. One of its blades hung down and was swaying in the breeze. That was the only movement they could see. The edged closer and as they came to the trunk they saw a lot of broken glass and two motionless bodies.

"Do you think they are dead?" Peter asked taking a step back.

"Only one way to find out," replied Mulwi and began to carefully climb the tree until he was level with the cockpit. He didn't need to check Anders' pulse as his neck was so broken he looked like a limp chicken. He did find a strong pulse on Easton's neck though. There were no apparent signs of serious injury and he began to free the belt and lowered him down to Peter and Max below.

"The other one is dead," Mulwi shouted.

"You get that fella inside and I'll cut this one down." Max swallowed hard as he thought of the dead man but there was nothing that they could do for him now. He recognised the guy that they were carrying from the service station on the M3. As they neared the house Max saw a shed at the back with a convenient looking chair in it. They sat the unconscious Easton into the chair and stepped back.

"Shouldn't we tie him up?" Peter asked.

"I guess you're right," replied Max and headed for the house for some rope. By the time Mulwi had returned with Anders' body over his shoulder Easton was well and truly bound to the chair.

"What you gonna do with him?" Mulwi asked slapping him on the back.

"I haven't worked that out yet," came the reply.

"Would a coldie help the thinking process?" smiled the tall aboriginal leading the way through the front door.

"Would it ever," replied Max wiping the sweat off his brow.

'Whoever tied these knots must have been a boy scout,' Easton thought as he wriggled in the chair. His eyes were adjusting slowly to the light though he could already tell that his present prison was made out of corrugated iron and had all manner of junk piled around the sides. Small holes and gaps in the sheeting let shafts of light in and it was almost as if he were being held captive in a colander. He remembered the crash

vaguely - the shot and the tree and then nothing. There was no sign of Anders.

'Where is he being kept?' he thought. Ironically if he'd been able to turn around he would have seen a dark blanket draped over his partner three feet behind him. It was musky and humid in this little shed and he was itching to wipe the beads of sweat off his nose. Where and who were their captors? He was pretty sure that it wouldn't be too long before he found out.

Mulwi sat fascinated, listening to Max's story explaining how they came to be in Australia and the chase that ended in his front garden. He was finishing an ice-cold beer and looked over at Max who had his hand under his chin in true contemplative pose. The other two were still cradling their beer bottles and Mulwi whispered to Peter.

"He always look like that when he's thinking?"

"Sometimes," Peter chuckled. Max got up slowly and walked to the fridge.

"Can I use some ice?" he said holding up a large piece.

"Yeah sure," Mulwi answered intrigued. "Can I do anything to help?" he asked eagerly.

"Actually you can," grinned Max.

The door of the shed creaked open slowly and the sun shone bright into Easton's face. He closed his eyes from the glare and squinted heavily. He could see the outline of the two figures in the doorway. One silhouette was surely Jones as it matched his bulky frame, but the other looked too tall to be his companion. The two figures entered and partially closed the door behind them. As the light dimmed he saw it was Jones but the man next to him was very dark skinned and distinctly tribal. He wore only a loin cloth and symbols were painted across his arms and chest. In this left hand he held an extremely sharp looking knife. In his right was a spear. They stood for a moment then Max spoke.

"Guess we are even," he said menacingly straight toward him.

"You're pal copped it in the helicopter and my mate Pete got crushed in the jeep." He spat out the words slowly and continued.

"So it's just you and me, and of course this fella here whose house you half destroyed," he said pointing to Mulwi who stood twirling the knife over and over in his hand.

"So you want to tell me what the hell's going on and why you guys want me dead?" Easton stayed silent and stared blankly ahead of him.

"I thought that'd be the case. Your choice buddy. OK Mulwi do your stuff."

Mulwi sneered and held up the knife. Easton shuddered a little to himself.

'Was Anders really dead? Were these two serious?'

"Oh I'm sorry, how rude of me," Max said, "I should explain what he's going to do," Max added, as Mulwi went out the door and returned with a box from which he produced a stone and began to grind the blade slowly and methodically.

"They have an ancient method of slicing pigs which involves razor thin cuts all along the animal while it still lives then letting it run wild. The cuts split wide as it runs and the adrenaline is said to spread throughout the meat." Max leaned closer and continued.

"The animal doesn't feel much until the last cut - so you have a while to choose to talk," he said and sat down on the ground near the door. Easton gritted his teeth as he felt Mulwi make the first incision. He could feel the cold edge of the blade on his skin and the drops of blood run down his back. Jones was right, there was not pain yet but the thought of the cut widening repulsed him. The second cut came and then the third. His determination to hold out was slowly ebbing away. He waited for the next cut but Mulwi came forward and ushered Max out of the door.

"What's the matter?" Max asked puzzled when they were out of earshot.

"All the ice has melted," Mulwi grinned.

"Do you think he's falling for it?" Max asked.

"He's heaps scared," Mulwi said, "but this will put him over the edge," he added, picking up a machete that he had on a hook by the back door. Max chuckled quietly to himself and waited for Mulwi to get some more ice from the kitchen.

"Sorry about that," Max said apologetically to Easton as he came back in through the shed door followed by Mulwi who began to slowly grind the machete.

"He decided he needed a bigger blade to do your shoulders," Max said with a nasty grin. Easton snapped and shouted.

"OK, OK, what do you want to know?"

"Why kill me?" Max replied quickly.

"You were getting too close at the hospital," Easton replied.

"So it was the CIA that set me up for McQuinn's murder," Max said shaking his head.

"All we were told was that McQuinn was a threat to the peace process and had to be erased. You had to be gotten out of the way too."

"Kill two birds with one stone eh?" Max mused.

"Something like that," said Easton.

"Do you know what they were doing at the hospital?" Max added.

"No," replied Easton, "except that it was some sort of research."

"Some research," said Max under his breath.

"Why not just get me sacked?" Max asked, "Why set me up?"

"Don't know," said Easton slowly. Max looked at their prisoner. He looked exhausted.

"Pete," he shouted out.

"Grab a few cold ones, our man here looks thirsty - oh and grab a towel too he's soaking wet." Max added.

"Towel?" Easton moaned.

"Yeah," said Mulwi, "this bloody ice melts so fast," he said running a cube over Easton's hands.

"You bastards!" Easton shouted and hung his head. Max chuckled then adopted a serious tone.

"Look I don't mean you any harm, and I'm sorry about your partner, that bit was true. I know you guys were only following orders," he said sympathetically.

'I wonder where Pete's got to,' he thought only to have two guns shoved in his face the moment he stepped out of the door. Pete was standing a few feet away and also had a pistol shoved in his ear.

"Tell your mate to come out with his hands on his head," said a stern voice. Before Max could say a word Mulwi was in front of them hands held high.

"His mate has pretty good hearing sir," he said as he took his place next to a worried looking Peter.

"Tom, do you want to go and free the prisoner," Sam said as he ushered Max next to Peter and Mulwi. Tom disappeared into the shed and quickly emerged with Easton and told him and the others to all sit on the edge of the back porch.

"Anders appears to have a broken neck," said Tom after a brief examination of the body.

"Would you mind me asking you who you guys are?" Easton asked wearily.

"We were coming to that," snapped Angie, "us 'guys' are internal affairs."

"Are these good guys or bad guys?" Mulwi asked Max.

"Good, I think. But then who am I to guess."

"Yes we are the good guys," Sam repeated.

"Can't we just arrest these two and then get back to the states," said Easton.

"Not so fast," said Angie, "We were in time to hear your little story."

"Under duress," Easton pleaded.

"Oh, yeah. Torture by ice cube. I'm sure that'll cut it with the chief!" said Tom.

'I walked into that one,' thought Easton cursing himself.

"Where do we go from here?" asked Max who wasn't sure if things had deteriorated or not.

"Where's your laptop?" Sam asked Easton.

"In the chopper I suppose," he replied and Tom set off to retrieve it. Sam whispered quietly to Angie.

"What do you think?"

"The visit to the doctor checked out. If we get Easton to call in then we'll get the full picture," Angie replied.

"My thoughts too, except don't mention Anders. They may get suspicious. I think the chief was right on this one. The smell is coming from way up."

"Yes, and I think we'd better cover our backs too." Angie said solemnly.

"I've disabled the emergency code just in case," said Tom as he returned with the laptop and briefcase.

"If you co-operate then we'll recommend they go very easy on you," said Sam. Easton nodded and keyed in his access code. Sam typed away and got the message ready for sending.

"Will it be re-routed?" asked Sam.

"I guess so. Yes" replied Easton.

Sam tutted and pulled out his mobile phone. He keyed in the long number and his access code and spoke quickly, "Agent X487329BY - Trace please on remote transmitter after it reaches central switchboard please. Transmission source? Alice

Springs, Australia. - Yes I'll hold". He motioned to Easton who keyed in his transmission code and waited.

"Thank you," said Sam and after a few moments.

"Copy of trace to Chief Jackson, internal affairs please."

"You mean you can trace any CIA transmission world-wide?" said Easton bewildered.

"Yep," replied Angie, "not even our big boss knows about that one," she said proudly.

"Looks like big brother has a big brother," Max chuckled.

"What now?" asked Peter.

"Well gentlemen," said Sam, "we wait to see what the person at the other end wants done," he pointed at the screen. They didn't wait too long before the message came up"

NEUTRALISE BOTH TARGETS. ERADICATE ALL TRACES OF ACTIVITY. FILE REPORT 'TARGETS COULD NOT BE LOCATED'. RETURN TO U.S. ASAP FOR DEBRIEF......

"According to this you have to waste these two innocent civilians and pretend that you never found them," said Sam to Easton.

"Does that mean that you're going to let him kill us?" said Peter in a worried voice.

"As far as the person at the other end is concerned you're already dead," smiled Angie.

Sam looked over at Angie and then back to the three civilians.

"You got room for two more lodgers?" Sam asked Mulwi pointing at Max and Peter.

"Yes Sir!" Mulwi answered with a sigh of relief.

"Just for a week or so while we go back and sort things out," Sam added.

"Am I a free man?" Max asked.

"It will take a few days to sort out a credible story for the British authorities. We'll send someone out to pick the two of you up and brief you," said Sam. "Oh and this should cover your expenses," he said handing Mulwi an envelope in which he carefully placed a number of notes. Max turned to Peter and wiped his hand across his brow.

As Tom and Angie walked around the side of the house helping Easton with the body of Anders, Max tapped Sam on the shoulder.

"Can I ask you a question?" he asked

"If it's about this case then the answer will probably be no," Sam replied.

"No. It's just curiosity really. Are you and that young lady, you know together?"

Sam stopped in his tracks and stared at Max.

"No," he replied quickly and then added, "Well, that is, it's not encouraged in our profession."

"Sod the profession," said Max. "I was lucky I got a second chance. I lost my first wife to my bloody profession. I may have been looking down the wrong end of a revolver for the last half an hour but even I could see the way the two of you look at each other."

Sam was stunned. He was being given personal advice by a man he had just met in very unusual circumstances. He paused for a moment and took a long look at Max. This man had been through a hell of a lot over the last few months and yet….. Sam held out his hand and shook Max's hard.

"Thanks," he said. "I guess I just had to hear it from a complete stranger."

Max smiled and reflected at the choice he had made all those years ago. *'Who knows what could have been,'* he thought. He then told himself not to be so silly and headed for the front of the house.

*** *** *** ***

The knocking on the door distracted him and instead of taking the congressman off hold he cut him off. *'He'll call back. They usually do,'* he thought. It had been a shitty day by all accounts and he'd been at his desk since 5am.

"Come in," he called out in a snappy irritated tone. The door opened to reveal Chief Jackson flanked by two MPs.

"Bob," he said surprised. "What a nice surprise."

"Not for me," came the reply. "Here's the warrant, read it," he added in a cold tone.

He placed the warrant on the desk. After a brief glance the man looked up.

"I'll have your balls for this," he shouted getting to his feet.

"We've got you, otherwise I wouldn't be here you dumbass. I know you have friends where it counts so keep you're mouth shut and face the music you composed," he snapped, surprised at his own confidence. He was, after all only internal affairs. The man behind the desk sat down slowly.

"I get my phone call I suppose," he said.

"Unfortunately, yes," came the reply.

*** *** *** ***

"What a waste of a good tea towel!" Peter laughed as Max paraded his new outfit.

"Very good," Mulwi laughed, "I'll have a word with the elders, maybe they'll let you become a temporary member of the tribe!" he laughed again.

"Remember this was your idea," Max reminded him as they set off for their walk in the bush all clothed in aboriginal dress. As close as they could get to traditional dress anyway. With only a bag full of beer over Peter's shoulder to link them to the modern world they set off at a moderate pace in respect for Max's convalescing leg.

"To really appreciate the beauty of the bush you have to get close to it." Mulwi said.

"Well my feet certainly are," Max grinned as he glanced down at his already dust-caked toes. The sun was still beating down and it was very hot.

"I walked this area and more when I was initiated as a young boy," said Mulwi.

"How long did you have to spend in the bush?" asked Peter.

"Three days," Mulwi said proudly. "Legend says you go into the bush as a boy and come back as a man."

"Return as a man with loads of blisters more like," Peter chuckled. The air was still and they heard the cackle of a nearby crow. They continued through the stunning scenery for about an hour when Mulwi realised his companions' feet weren't up to much more.

"Here we stop to make a fire before it gets colder," he announced. They actually had ages before the sunset but these two would struggle to get to the next suitable spot. Both Max and Peter sighed with relief and gladly collected the necessary firewood to create a good blaze. They cracked open a beer and Max and Peter listened intently while Mulwi described the 'boat race' they ran every summer in the river that runs through Alice Springs.

"There is, of course, no water in the river at that time of year and the boats have no bottom to them to allow the competitors' feet to run along the ground. They run through the sand carrying the boat between the team of them," he explained.

"That doesn't sound too hard," Max commented.

"Except that to qualify to be in one of the teams you have to drink a whole case of beer beforehand," Mulwi added. "Have you ever tried to run through baking hot sand after that much grog?" he teased.

"Come to think of it I did try and run along Brighton beach after six pints once," Max laughed, "but I didn't get very far." They took turns telling drinking stories and despite being the youngest Peter kept them amused with how he and his girlfriend had woken up with fourteen 'For Sale' signs in her front garden after one of his nights out and various other antics from his university days in Bristol. After a dozen or so bottles had returned to the bag empty, Mulwi attempted to lead them in a traditional aboriginal song. After the somewhat poor performance he shook his head.

"Every frog for many miles will descend on us after that," he laughed.

"So smug," smiled Max, "I thought you might pull a stunt like that, so I took the liberty of bringing along a tune that suits my deep tones much better," he smirked as he got a couple of pieces of paper on which he had written the words for his two friends.

"I hope this will be a rendition of which The King himself would be proud. I'll do one verse then you can copy," he said and Peter smiled and winked at Mulwi who winked back. They both knew the song but didn't want to miss out on hearing Max's solo. They were pleasantly surprised as their large comrade hit every note. Well almost. When he finished they clapped and cheered enough to make him blush. They cleared their throats and Max counted them in.......

'As the snow flies,
On a cold and grey Chicago morn,
Another little bay child is born, in the Ghetto,
And his momma cries....'

The three voices, accompanied by the crackling fire, drifted across the plains. A bush-tailed possum paused briefly at the sight and sound.

'They must be standing too close to that fire,' he thought and scurried off into the night.

**** **** **** ****

There was that knocking again. Max decided to face the fact that there was someone at the door. He could hear two voices, too, but not what they were saying. To quote Mulwi he had 'a family of kangaroos living in his head' at the moment. His mouth tasted awful and he guessed his breath wouldn't be all that much better. He hauled himself off the floor where he had thrown himself in the early hours. The walk back had been much easier than the one into the bush. At least he thought so, he wasn't altogether sure. He was about to open the door when he realised he was still in 'tribal costume' and dug around for a shirt. Mulwi and Peter were both still asleep. Unconscious would be more accurate. He ran his fingers through his hair and checked his breath. Bad, bad move. *'Oh well,'* he thought and opened the door. The two smart young gentlemen seemed shocked at the sight before them.

"Mr Jones?" one of them asked tentatively.

"Yeah, for my sins," Max smiled.

"Ah, we've erm, come to debrief you and escort you back to the U.K," the smaller one said.

"OK lads I'll put the kettle on," he replied fumbling.

"We've just had one thank you, sir," said the other. "We have an eight berth roadster nearby. The boss decided we would drive you down to Sydney and brief you on the way there. Is that OK with you?" he added politely.

"Oh sure, whatever. If you can give us a few minutes," Max said.

"Certainly," they choroused, and both turned and headed back toward the road. Fifteen minutes of frantic tidying themselves up and packing and Max and Peter were on the front steps saying goodbye to Mulwi.

"Thanks for everything," Max said. "You've been a mate," he added as he shook Mulwi's hand hard.

"No worries," he grinned. "Besides, with the money they gave me to fix my wall I'll be set for grog for about six months," he laughed. Peter said his goodbyes and the two of them walked up the road to the campervan.

**** **** **** ****

By the time they reached Sydney in a little over three days and nights driving, they had their version of events down to a tee. Max's relief at being both alive and free overwhelmed the annoyance and anger at having to adopt the agency's cover up. He'd been little placated by the assurance that those responsible had been 'appropriately dealt with'. Whatever that meant. His return to work had been assured, with a hefty promotion. Max kept his word to Peter who had already begun work on the story and sent word ahead to England. News had also been sent to both of their families and they could look forward to a warm welcome at Heathrow airport. They were sitting in the departure lounge at Sydney and Max was indulging in a bit of reflection. Peter was engrossed in the Sydney Morning Herald.

'A long way round of getting to see a bit of the world,' Max observed. He was looking forward to seeing his wife again. Although they had little in common and led fairly independent lives, they had had a good marriage. He made a mental note to take her away for a while when he got back. Peter tapped him on the shoulder and handed him the newspaper. It was open at the 'World' section and Peter had circled a certain story.

'WASHINGTON BUDGET NEWS- Following the death of the President at 3:27am Eastern Standard Time on Thursday, the major departments in the government have been rocked with news of funding cuts. The vice president Mr. Henry Forbes was sworn in immediately and as expected wasted no time re-enforcing his personal tough stance on public spending. With an election only a month away he vowed the axe would fall quickly on a number of departments. Defence and the internal agencies are expected to be hardest hit. It has come as a particularly cruel blow to the new director of the CIA, Dan Myers, who has only been in the job three days following last week's sudden resignation of his predecessor. Both the president and his Republican opponent had been in favour of additional security funding. Had the president made it to the election, Myers would have taken over the most prolific internal agency in the world whatever the result. Instead, he faces an uphill struggle. President Forbes defended his tough stance, so soon after the president's death from a brain haemorrhage, saying that the world needed to know a strong man was at the head of the world's most powerful economic nation in the midst of a global recession. Critics have argued that it is purely a vote winning ploy to reverse gains by the republicans in recent opinion polls...................'

The End

Cuban Cut

&

Cut To The Chase

are both available as e-books in Palm™ and PDF formats with the help of DigitalWrite – links to e-bookshops from www.cubancut.com

Details of opportunities for other UK writers are available at www.mxpublishing.com

This book was written by Steve Emecz and is representative of a completely digital workflow. It was created, proofed, printed and finally stored digitally for future on demand reprints.

The covers were printed on the DocuColor 2060 using Xerox Colortech paper. The text was imposed using Preps software and then printed using Xerox Publisher paper on the DocuTech Book Factory. The covers were introduced and the 3 knife trim completed the story, if you see what I mean.

Please enjoy this complimentary copy.